"Did you feel something just then?"

Kate asked in a hushed tone. "When I... When you..."

"When we kissed?" Darren finished for her.

"Yes."

"I felt like this," he said, pulling her to him. He put his hands on her shoulders and lowered his mouth to hers.

This time there was no accidental brushing of lips. He kissed her with everything he had, taking her mouth with gentle persuasion and making it his.

He kissed her until she swayed against him. She let her hands climb to his chest and link behind his back. Maybe they couldn't indulge in anything too sexual in a public park, but foreplay could take all sorts of forms.

She reached for a grape and slipped it between his lips. "When we get home, you'll get your real dessert."

Dear Reader,

I don't know about you, but I'm fascinated by those reality TV shows where people are in public dating contests to win the rich guy or gal. I always wonder about the men and women who are drawn to do that sort of thing. Naturally, as a writer, once you start wondering about people you begin to create characters who might find themselves in a certain situation. What if the "prize catch" was unwilling and had been manipulated into being a celebrity bachelor?

A theme that I explore a lot in my books is appearance versus reality. Most of us create images of ourselves that we project to the world. Sometimes these are very close to the "real" us and sometimes quite different. What if my celebrity bachelor ran away from his unwanted fame and chose a disguise that was a lot truer to who he really is? What if he ended up falling for a woman completely different to the woman he thought he wanted? And what if this one didn't fall at his feet?

Darren and Kate were a lot of fun to write about. I hope you enjoy their story.

For info on my upcoming releases, contests and to join my e-mail fan group, come visit me at www.nancywarren.net.

Happy reading,

Nancy Warren

NANCY WARREN

UNDERNEATH IT ALL

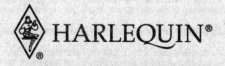

HARLEQUIN®

TORONTO • NEW YORK • LONDON
AMSTERDAM • PARIS • SYDNEY • HAMBURG
STOCKHOLM • ATHENS • TOKYO • MILAN • MADRID
PRAGUE • WARSAW • BUDAPEST • AUCKLAND

This book is dedicated to Robin Taylor:
a voracious reader, supportive fan, thoughtful reviewer
and all-around nice person.
Thanks for everything, Robin.

ISBN 0-373-69187-4

UNDERNEATH IT ALL

Copyright © 2004 by Nancy Warren.

1

DARREN KAISER was literally on top of the world. He was chatting to one of the hottest-looking women—and there was stiff competition—at a rooftop cocktail reception in Manhattan.

"I'll call you," Darren Kaiser's new friend, Serena, said, her shoulder-length blond hair swinging against athletically sculpted shoulders perfectly displayed in a clingy black halter dress. She leaned forward to give Darren a kiss that promised a lot more than phone conversation.

"You do that," he said, giving her a kiss back that let her know he could keep up his end of whatever she had in mind. From the rooftop deck, all of New York City was laid out in noisy, sparkling splendor, far beneath the well-heeled feet of upwardly mobile twenty- and thirty-somethings.

He nodded to a couple of acquaintances, then decided he'd stayed long enough. He pulled out his cell phone to call his car service for a pickup, then slowed to redrape a sexy young woman's shawl over her shoulder from whence it had dropped. She rewarded him with a blindingly white smile and an air kiss.

Not being much of an air-kisser himself, he winked at her and kept going.

Darren Kaiser loved being a single man in Manhattan. There were so many beautiful, smart, sexy women. He was crazy about the new female power-babes who were totally up-front about what they wanted, when they wanted it and with whom.

Especially when they wanted it with him.

He whistled as he left Studio 450, where the benefit for fibromyalgia was still in full swing. The benefit was a thinly veiled excuse for singles to check one another out. Darren was here on a corporate ticket paid for by Kaiser Image Makers, and he still felt as if he was working, since he was expected to hand out a few business cards and schmooze.

So, he'd schmoozed a beautiful woman. Or, more accurately, she'd schmoozed him. These days, a man didn't even need to take a pen and paper with him to the dating-and-mating hunting grounds. If a woman was interested, she'd do what Serena had done—pull out her Palm Pilot and enter him into her database.

Thoughts of the sexy Serena almost made Darren contemplate blowing off work tonight. But he was anxious to get a few hours in—before his pseudo work in the morning. He'd found a glitch in the educational software program he was designing and he'd suddenly had an idea for how to fix it right about the time he sipped his first martini and chomped his first hors d'oeuvres.

He'd have bolted home right then, except that Serena had appeared with a toss of blond hair, an it's-your-lucky-night smile and her hand extended.

He'd enjoyed chatting with her and exchanging speculative eye contact, enjoyed the first few steps of a dance he never tired of: the dance of seduction. Unlike the bulk of Manhattanites, old and young, she hadn't wanted to talk exclusively about herself. Serena Ashcroft had seemed genuinely interested in him. His politics, his tastes in fashion, music, movies, clothes and women. Not being stupid, he'd described his ideal woman as someone a lot like Serena. He'd looked into her cool, patrician blue eyes and said, "My ideal woman is blonde, articulate, slim and sexy, and isn't afraid to go after what she wants." He leaned closer so he could smell her expensive scent. "Especially when what she wants is me." She'd looked so enthralled with his answers he almost expected her to take notes.

Still whistling, he jumped into the black limo that pulled up just as he hit the pavement, wondering how long it would take Serena to call.

Serena was pale, blonde and patrician—the sort of woman whose ancestors had traveled over on the *Mayflower*. His forbears had come over steerage-class—if they hadn't stowed away—on some overcrowded European steamer. Their first taste of America hadn't been Plymouth Rock, but Ellis Island.

He felt his blood quicken as he challenged himself to prove to this sexy blonde that he was worthy. He loved a challenge.

As he'd expected, Serena called, not the next day, but the day after, and suggested they meet for a drink after work. And for the next couple of months, they got together sporadically. They never seemed able to coordinate their schedules for serious dating, but he was busy, anyway.

She was in publishing, she told him, and he imagined

her editing the memoirs of famous men and women of letters. It was an occupation that would suit her.

A couple of times they were photographed by one or other of the paparazzi that hopped around the social scene like fleas. As a VP and son of the CEO of one of the hottest ad agencies in town, Darren was used to the attention, but usually tried to blow it off. Serena seemed to enjoy having her photo taken when they were together, however, so he put up and shut up, knowing that his father would get a thrill seeing the company name mentioned in print and his son's picture in the paper.

Then, one warm late spring day, Darren discovered Serena had set him up.

The day started as it usually did. Tired from working too late the night before at his computer, he grabbed a java from the corner coffee shop he frequented on Madison Avenue half a block from his office.

He gulped the dark, liquid caffeine, hoping it would jump-start his sleep-deprived brain, as he tried to concentrate on today's tasks. He was expecting focus-group results on a campaign for a new soda; he was increasing the TV buy for a sportswear manufacturer; and he was booked to have lunch with a prospective client.

The crowded elevator rose and let him out on his floor, the upper of the three levels that housed Kaiser Image Makers, which most people referred to simply as KIM.

"Congratulations, Darren," said Angie, the receptionist, before answering a ringing phone.

He sent her a wave, wondering why she was offering kudos. Had he done something good? He tried to recall what it was. Hopefully it would be enough to please the old man.

Sure enough, when he got to his office, his father was standing in front of Darren's gleaming white desk, his smile as glossy as the magazine in his hands. Was it *Advertising Age?* Positive industry buzz always excited his publicity hound of a father. But no, the magazine was a regular-size one with a young, dark-haired man on the cover. Must be some successful ad campaign that had his dad licking his chops.

"Hey, Dad. How's it going?"

"Congratulations, son. I knew you didn't turn out good-looking like your mother for nothing." And his father, president, CEO and founder of KIM closed the magazine and thrust it toward Darren.

Darren stared at the cover, and the bottom of his stomach went into free fall. "What the..." His words felt sucked dry as though a vacuum hose had attacked his mouth, taking the breath out of his body.

The mug grinning up at him from the front cover of *Matchmaker* magazine—nationwide circulation in the millions—was his. And the headline over the top read, "Manhattan Match of the Year, Advertising Executive, Darren Kaiser."

Darren flopped onto the black Bauhaus couch as his legs gave out on him.

"What..." He tried to pull air into his lungs, but they felt flattened. He tried again. "How did they..." Finally he reached out a hand. "Let me see that."

His father chuckled as though he were Santa Claus and this was Christmas Eve. He was smoking a cigar, which his cardiologist had forbade him, and his laugh-

ter shook the seventy or so plus pounds he was supposed to shed.

"I wasn't certain they'd pick you. But I was very per-
suasive." His dad chuckled again, happier than Darren
had seen him in months.

"Pick me for what?" Darren asked, knowing he
didn't want to hear the answer.

"Where have you been, boy? I keep telling you
you've got to stay on top of popular media if you're going to make it in advertising. This Match of the Year
thing is huge. It's like *People*'s Sexiest Man on Earth—
which reminds me, we'll have to send them some hints
to look your way now you're going to be so famous."

The thought of conducting his love life in public
made him nauseous.

"Darren, your mother and I want nothing more than
to see you settle down and marry a nice girl. Now that
the magazine has decided you're a great catch, there'll
be all kinds of publicity. You could date royalty, movie
stars. Anybody!"

"No."

"I want grandchildren."

"You'll have to wait."

"You don't have to marry any of them if you don't
want to. You just play the game. You'll be famous, KIM
will be famous. Clients will pour out of the wood-
work."

"I am not putting my love life on display so you can
make a few more million. No."

"Think of the publicity. You'll be photographed everywhere, you'll get pretty girls proposing, all of America will be part of your courtship." The old man's eyes

twinkled with excitement. "Think what the reality TV show did for that tire fellow."

"They broke up." A shudder shook Darren as he imagined his love life as a reality TV show. At least the magazine thing wasn't that bad. Swiftly, his media-savvy brain assessed the damage as he tried to convince himself this Match of the Year pick wasn't a total, life-altering disaster.

All at once the most obvious objection sprang to mind. "This is a nightmare. I can't believe the media group that owns *Matchmaker* magazine would choose me without my knowledge or consent. I mean, this is an invasion of privacy right here. Where did they even get this picture?" He jabbed a finger at the photograph. "That was taken at our company's annual general meeting last year." He flipped a page angrily and saw an even worse sight. "And where the hell did they get my baby picture?" he yelled.

His father chuckled, sending out a puff of cigar smoke.

And in that moment he knew. "Dad."

He and his father rarely saw eye to eye, but he'd never wanted to deck dear old dad until now. "You gave that photo to them. Didn't you?"

"Of course I did. We wanted this to be a surprise. You weren't the only possible candidate, you know. Men all over America would kill to be in your shoes."

"Who's 'we'?"

"That pleasant young woman who's the special-assignment editor for *Matchmaker* magazine. Serena Ashcroft. There's a picture of the two of you together in the four-page spread." Darren Kaiser Sr. jabbed his cigar toward the magazine. "You can't buy that kind of publicity."

Darren flipped none too gently through the pages until he saw even more photos of him at various events, with an assortment of women, including Serena of the big blue eyes and the "Oh, let's talk about you," conniving personality.

He'd talked, and she'd either recorded their conversations or she had a damn good memory. There he was, revealed in photographs and print in all his glory. His tastes in everything from music to restaurants laid out for all the world to dine on.

My ideal woman, jumped out at him. They'd displayed this little gem of wisdom in a text box with a larger type size.

My ideal woman is a blonde. She's a professional woman who knows what she wants from life and isn't afraid to go after it. Even if that something is me. She's educated, intelligent, classy, but also very sexy.

Sweat was starting to dampen his brow and he felt like he might puke. He didn't doubt he'd spouted that nonsense, but he'd never intended it for any ears but Serena's.

A quick skim told him that there was a Web site where women could write in about themselves and why they would love to date Darren. Since the magazine pledged to do its best to fix him up with eligible women throughout the year, there would be updates about his dating habits, his preferences and his experiences with the opposite sex.

He was having trouble turning the pages and he realized even his fingertips had started to sweat.

"Darren," his assistant, Jeanie, called breathlessly from his doorway. "I'm sorry to interrupt, but I've got *The Tonight Show* people on line one and *Entertainment Tonight* holding on line two."

"Wonderful. Wonderful," said his father. "I'll let you go, then."

"Dad, what have you done?" Darren asked hoarsely.

"What our company does best, son. I've given you an image as the most eligible bachelor in America."

KATE MONAHAN'S FEET ACHED, which wasn't surprising since she'd been on them all day. She was halfway through her third twelve-hour shift at New Image, the salon where she worked, in as many days. But her younger brother, Huey, needed braces and she had her eye on a DKNY skirt and jacket that her bargain-hunter nose told her was headed for another markdown, so she tried to think about her bank balance and not her feet.

Graduation season was always a busy, and lucrative, time of year.

"So," she said to her fourth high-school senior that day, "what are we doing?"

"I want it layered, you know, like Rachel in *Friends*."

"Sure."

"But with the fluttery bangs like Cameron Diaz in *Charlie's Angels*. Not the first movie but the second one."

"Aha." She shifted feet, trying to get the ache out of her lower back. Her friend and co-worker, Ruby, breezed by and they exchanged a glance, but at least her friend didn't say anything to make her laugh. With Ruby, you could never tell.

"And the same color as Julianne Moore, only more like Julia Roberts in *Pretty Woman*."

"You're going to dye your hair for grad?"

It never failed to amaze Kate what these girls' mothers let them get away with.

"Yep. Well, like your hair. What color is that?" the teenager with perfectly attractive brown hair asked her with a squint that was assessing. "Mocha berry or copper glitz?"

Kate grabbed a fistful of the mass of curls that no styling product, blow dryer or curling iron could ever entirely tame. "It's red, and it's the color God gave me."

"Well, God gave me this boring brown and I want to look as hot as you when I graduate."

Kate sent soon-to-graduate Bethany off to be shampooed and quickly phoned the girl's mother to make sure it was okay about the color. *Anything she wants*, was the answer.

At eighteen. Imagine.

Ruby stopped her and said, "Tell that girl that Ashton Kutcher has cuter bangs. And no haircut or dye job is going to make her look like Julia Roberts."

She stifled a giggle, but Ruby was right. Still, it didn't hurt to put a little magic in a young woman's life. She'd do what she could.

Once she had Bethany settled under the dryer, she passed her a sheaf of current magazines, and the brunette, soon-to-be-redhead immediately chose a well-thumbed copy of *Matchmaker* magazine.

"If I could marry him," the girl said, pointing a freshly manicured index finger at the photo on the cover, "I'd be set for life."

Kate gazed at the man's picture. "Darren Kaiser, *Matchmaker*'s Match of the Year," she read, staring at the man deemed so eligible women would go to humiliating lengths to marry him.

Darren Kaiser had *playboy* written all over him. He had Brad Pitt blond hair, a little long and with just a hint of a curl at the ends. It looked as though each strand had been individually groomed to provide that tousled disorder. He had the sensual face of a man who likes women and usually gets whatever he wants from them. His lips tilted in a smile that was only going through the motions—there was no genuine warmth. Beautiful eyes, she thought, but cynical. He wore a suit, and even though only the shoulders were visible in the picture, she was certain the clothes on his back cost more than her mother spent to feed her family for a year.

Yes, she thought, he was good-looking in a smooth, slick sort of way, but she didn't see a real man in the photo. More like a perfect image of one.

"He's a hottie," sighed her client.

"He looks altogether too full of himself. And those rich men—" Kate shook her head "—what would they want with the likes of us? We'd end up picking up their socks and propping up their egos. Bethany, take my advice and find yourself a decent man who cares about you. Leave the boy millionaires to marry girl millionaires."

She glanced at the photo of Brian she'd taped to her station. He was so different from the glossy fellow with the perfect smile. Things had been a bit weird lately between her and her boyfriend, but she thought it was because they were both so busy right now. Brian would never be a magazine cover's idea of the ideal bachelor, but he was a down-to-earth man with a steady job in banking who shared her basic values.

He was ambitious, too, which was good. Having grown up with a widowed mother and four brothers and sisters, lack of money was all too familiar. Kate appreciated an ambitious man with a steady job. Besides, with all his training and knowledge, Brian was investing her money for her so she could achieve her dreams more quickly.

She glanced at the about-to-graduate teen glued to the story of a fantasy man and shook her head. No glossy hunk on a magazine cover was going to drop into their lives and provide the happily-ever-after.

2

"I QUIT!" Darren yelled, almost as red-faced as his father. "I can't take this anymore. Women are waiting outside my co-op when I leave in the morning. Women are hanging around outside the office with signs written in lipstick reading, "Choose me!"

"You're exag—"

"I've been propositioned, stalked, proposed to about three thousand times. This morning the doorman handed me a woman's bra with a phone number on it."

"It's the excitement of the magazine, son." His father tried to sound sympathetic, but he was as gleeful as a boy with a new Hot Wheels set. "A few months from now they'll have forgotten all about you."

"Not if you can help it," he mumbled.

"We'll hire you a bodyguard," his dad replied.

"I don't want a bodyguard. I want my life back."

In fact, what he wanted was his life. His own life. Forget the family business, he wanted to succeed or fail on his own terms. Doing something he loved a lot more than creating artificial "need" in the marketplace for products anyone could live without.

"Our business has gone way up in the past week. Think of what this could mean."

"No. Dad. I'm thinking about me. I love programming, it's what I want to do with my life. Face it, I'm a computer geek and I don't belong in advertising. I'm quitting. As of now."

Their voices were rising, but Darren didn't care. He'd inherited his temper from his father, if nothing else.

Just as angry, his father shouted, "You walk out that door, young man, and you can't change your mind."

"I won't." Darren strode across the room but hesitated at the doorway of his dad's plush office, feeling not so much fear for his own future, but worry that his father couldn't cope without him. He was about to speak when he heard some sort of commotion down the hall in the direction of his own office.

He turned and swallowed an expletive. There was a camera crew in front of his office, and damned if they weren't filming some woman, some complete and utter stranger, leaving a dozen red roses outside his door. She was talking all the time, her face toward the camera so the flowers almost got knocked to the floor.

Oh, no. This had gone far enough. His dad had turned his life and his job into a joke. He'd become, not an ad exec, but a product to be marketed. The hell with it. Kaiser Image Makers would survive without Darren.

And Darren was going to be fine without Kaiser.

But before he left, he was going to give that woman and the cameraman a piece of his mind. Angrily, he made his way toward them. Instead of looking guilty and hurrying away, the woman with the roses, beamed a thousand-watt smile his way, then shouted into the camera, "There he is!"

She picked up the roses, yelled, "These are for you, Darren Kaiser. I love you," and headed his way, hampered by her red stilettos and body-hugging red dress.

She was followed by a skinny guy in a Knicks shirt balancing a TV camera on his shoulder.

In a moment of horror, Darren realized that unless he disappeared fast, whatever happened next would be filmed. He abandoned his plans to dress down the camera guy and the misguided woman. He abandoned any thoughts of standing his ground.

He turned on his heel and ran.

KIM employees stood in the hallway, mesmerized, until Darren yelled, "Out of my way," and set a world sprinting record racing for the stairwell.

He was out of here.

Running on instinct, he tore down several flights of stairs, spurred by the sounds of pursuit far above. Then he abruptly stopped and, as quietly as possible, opened the door to the twelfth floor and the law offices of Stoat, Remington, Bryce, where his buddy Bart worked. Since the receptionist knew him, she motioned him to go on through.

"You never saw me," he panted, and, ignoring her startled expression, kept going, racing through the hallowed halls of the law offices to seek temporary shelter with his old friend.

Stumbling into Bart's office without knocking, he shut the door, put his sunglasses on and borrowed the Yankees baseball cap Bart kept hanging on his wall along with a signed pennant. Then he slouched low in the leather club chair Bart kept for office visitors.

"Drop in anytime," Bart said as he watched Darren.

"I'm in trouble."

"Hey," Bart complained, as Darren tugged on the cap. "You can't wear that! You're a Giants fan."

"I'm in serious trouble, Bart." Darren panted, expecting any second to hear the sounds of that crazy female after him like a baying hound after a juicy fox.

"You have to help me."

As well as being a good friend, Bart was a dedicated lawyer. He immediately assumed an air of concern. "You did the right thing coming here. What's up?"

"I quit my job just now and I have to get out of town. Go far away where no one has ever heard of *Matchmaker*."

Bart's expression of concern was replaced with one of hastily suppressed amusement. "Is that what your trouble is?"

"Yes! It's that magazine."

"I don't want to make your day any worse, old buddy, but you're everywhere. It's not just the magazine. It's the Internet, chat groups, newspapers and on the TV. You, my friend, are news."

"I need to stop being news. Damn it, I never agreed to be Match of the Year. I want to sue Matchmaker Enterprises or whatever they call themselves, Bart."

"What for?"

"You're my lawyer. Aren't you supposed to advise me? How about defamation of character? Harassment? Libel?"

"Buddy, they aren't defaming you when they call you God's gift to women. It's supposed to be a compliment."

"I can't even live in peace in my own home. I'm being mobbed, stalked. Women I don't know give me their bras. Mary Jane Lancer proposed." He'd known Mary Jane for years. Their fathers belonged to the same club.

She was part of his social circle, but there never had been a hint of attraction between them until the bachelor thing.

A rich chuckle answered him. "Harassment. Hmm. There are men all over America who would kill to be in your shoes. You'd only make a fool of yourself."

There was a long pause. Darren waited while Bart drummed his fingers on his blotter, obviously deep in thought.

"But libel, now you've got something. Let's see, I just happen to have a copy of the magazine." He twirled his chair and found the hated magazine in a stack of papers and flipped it open. "Ah, here it is. They called you rich, good-looking and intelligent. Man, we can sue for millions."

Darren's heart sank. "Okay, very funny. So what do I do?"

"My best advice is to go with the flow. Have fun with it. Make your father's company a few more millions. Enjoy your fifteen minutes of fame and kiss a bunch of gorgeous women. Seriously, have you seen the babes who go for stuff like this? Be the rich boy all the girls want to marry. It'll be over in a year and long before that somebody else will be news."

"You don't get it. It's not just me being a minor celebrity and that's it. A week ago I was a happy single man living a wonderful single life. I was a New York bachelor. One of millions. Now I'm some freakin' great catch and no one but no one thinks I should remain a happy bachelor."

He paused to take a breath and a quick check outside Bart's office. So far he seemed safe.

"In the past week, I have been proposed to by girls with braces, women old enough to be my mother, loonies, the lonely, the desperate, and even women I thought were my friends, Like Mary Jane Lancer." That, he thought, had been the worst. "It's like they're trying to snap me up before any other woman gets a chance."

Bart started to chuckle. "Let me get this straight. Are you telling me you don't want women all over the country throwing themselves at you? Is that what I'm hearing?"

"Yes! I told Serena Ashcroft I won't cooperate. They should admit they made a mistake and find someone else. She told me to think about it. No hurry. I told her I won't change my mind and she laughed."

"I'm sure they would stop writing about you if you won't cooperate. They have the right to choose you as the most eligible bachelor, though. You can't stop them loving you."

"I don't know. She's a devious woman. Who knows what she's planning? I can't stand it anymore."

Bart shrugged. "Do what movie stars do when they want some privacy. Hide. Lay low somewhere until this blows over."

"Hide?"

"Sure. If you insist on trying to avoid publicity, why don't you pretend you're in the Witness Protection Program? Find a new locale, a new identity. Maybe a disguise."

Bart had enjoyed a brief spell of fame in college as an actor. Particularly memorable had been his Falstaff. Truly a method actor, he'd become roaring drunk every

night for weeks before the performance in order to prepare for the role. He'd been good, too. Except that his
brain had been so alcohol-saturated and his hangover
so severe, that he'd forgotten half his lines on opening
night.

What Bart was suggesting was that Darren run away.
He'd never been the type to run from his problems, but
suddenly it seemed as though he were being offered
freedom, the likes of which he'd never known.

He sat up, slipping his sunglasses down his nose so
he could regard his friend more clearly. "If I hide out
somewhere, I can take some time to work on my own
stuff." Not having to sneak in his real work at night
would be incredible. He had some money saved up,
and if he sold his BMW he would have some decent
cash quickly, enough to live on for a while. He could
probably finish his line of software programs in less
than a year.

"Right. You're the next Bill Gates. I forgot."

Darren didn't bother to correct him. He had one line
of educational software he was developing to help kids
read. His younger brother Eric had a symbol-retrieval
problem and he'd found a way to help him by writing a
simple program. Eric was now studying engineering at
college—and the fact that he'd made the difference in
his younger bro's life gave him a lot more pride and satisfaction than his most successful day at the family firm.
Now he wanted to see if he could create a more elabo-
rate program that might help other kids like his brother.

Maybe his program wouldn't cure cancer, but helping kids overcome learning hurdles felt more useful to

him than getting some KIM client's brand of deodorant
up two percentage points in the marketplace.

"Okay. But you've got to help me."

Bart grinned. "You have come to the right place," he
said, almost rubbing his hands with glee. "You're one
of the most famous faces in America. But, my man,
we're about to change all that." Bart, the sometime actor, rose majestically from behind his desk and gestured. "Follow me," he said. After a surreptitious
glance up and down the hallway, they surmised the
coast was clear, then took the elevator to the main floor.

After hiding in the back seat while Bart drove them
out of the building's car park, Darren wondered how
famous people handled celebrity. He felt hunted, and
the baseball cap and dark glasses, not to mention the
Brooks Brothers suit, weren't helping him blend in with
the crowd.

They ended up in a drugstore, where Bart pondered a
row of Miss Clairol boxes. "You want to blend in with
the locals, but look completely different from how you
look now. Where are you going, anyway?"

Maybe it was the throwaway comment about Bill
Gates, but it made up Darren's mind. "Seattle."

"That's a long way away."

"Exactly. I don't know anyone there, I've no reason to
go. Hell, I was only there once for a weekend. No one
will think to look for me in Seattle."

Bart picked up a box of dark brown hair dye.

"What are we doing in the girl aisle?"

"Women's hair dye doesn't last as long as the men's
stuff," Bart explained, reading the instructions on the
box as though he might actually need them.

"I'm not dying my hair."

"Do you want to disappear or don't you?"

"Yes. But..." He stared at the box. "If I wear Miss Clairol, I might as well pierce my ears and wear pink golf shirts."

Bart snapped his fingers. "Now, that's a great—"

"Forget it."

"Listen, here's some advice from a once potentially great actor. If you want to become a character, you step into his shoes and into his skin."

"And into their hair dye. Yeah. I've got it."

"It's not just his hair. It's the whole persona. What we're doing is building a character. Who is this man who's going to appear in Seattle? We'll start with the hair and see where it goes."

A woman glanced at them curiously and then picked up a box with a picture of a blonde on it.

Darren stood there surrounded by women's hair-styling products, wondering how his life had ever come to this. Finally, he pulled out his wallet and handed Bart a twenty.

"You're buying it."

Two hours later, they were at Bart's place and his damp hair was now brown. Darren couldn't believe how it changed his appearance. His skin tone seemed lighter, his eyes darker.

"I've been thinking," said Bart, who was getting right into this dye-your-hair and dress-up thing. "You really are a computer geek, and you'll be living in Silicon Valley north, so why not dress like one? It's the perfect disguise."

"What, you mean wear plastic pocket protectors and plaid weenie shirts?"

"Too much?"

"Definitely."

"Okay. The trick is to keep people's attention off your face. I've got some black thick-framed glasses from when I played Willy Loman. They'd be perfect. The hair, baseball caps, those will help. But I'm thinking wild shirts like boarders wear. Loud, casual and cheap." His buddy laughed and then clapped him on the back.

"Geek chic."

Darren snorted. But he kind of liked the idea. Who'd look for him under a loud shirt? He'd never owned such a thing in his life.

"Okay," he said, knowing he couldn't pass up this opportunity to escape being marriage bait and at the same time follow his private dream. "I'll do it."

"Great." Bart dug in a drawer for a pair of kitchen shears. "Now, hold still," he said, and picked up a lump of Darren's still-damp hair.

"I paid two hundred bucks to have my hair cut two weeks ago," Darren informed his old buddy.

"Welcome to the world of—hey, what are you going to call yourself?" Bart asked as he started cutting.

KATE MONAHAN SAT AT HER kitchen table with her calculator and her monthly budget. She had the pleasant feeling of being ahead of her target.

She'd worked a lot of extra shifts to get here, but knowing her investment account with Brian's bank was growing, and that soon she'd be able to follow her lifelong dream and enroll in teacher's college, had her beaming.

She heard the broken cement at the end of the duplex's driveway rattle as a car rolled in. The landlord was too cheap to fix the drive, or much else, but the rent was reasonable so she didn't complain. She wondered if this could be the new tenant moving in upstairs, and got up to look out the window.

She hoped it would be someone as friendly as the last tenant, Annie.

Kate went to the kitchen window and peeked out. Well, it was a guy moving in. Annie had been a fun-loving flight attendant—a girl after Kate's heart—and the house had been more like a single home than a duplex. But Annie had been transferred to Denver. Somehow, Kate didn't think this guy and she were going to be watching old movies together and sharing bowls of popcorn, or borrowing shoes and jackets.

He got out of a nondescript beige compact that had seen better days and glanced around as though suspecting he might have been followed.

The guy was tall, and he stretched his back as though he'd been driving a long time, pulled off the baseball cap he wore low over his eyes and scratched his scalp. He had dark brown hair in a cut his barber ought to be ashamed of, glasses with thick black frames on a pleasant, strong-boned face. He looked sort of familiar, though she was certain they'd never met. But it was hard to concentrate on his face when he was wearing such a wild shirt. Bright red, with big white flowers. The shirt was open to expose a white T-shirt that was soft from many washings. He wore creased cargo shorts and navy flip flops.

Shoving the cap back on his head, he popped open the trunk and pulled out a computer keyboard and a cardboard box with computer-type stuff sticking out and started toward the outside stairs that led up to his suite. Suddenly, he stopped, his gaze focusing on her kitchen window.

Her hair. It must be her wretched hair that had caught his attention. She'd thought she was hiding behind her curtains, but obviously he'd caught sight of her.

Well, she'd have to introduce herself now.

She opened the kitchen door and stepped out. "Hi," she said, with a friendly smile.

He nodded. Not smiling. Not speaking. Looking at her as though she might be an assassin sent to kill him. Oh, great. He looked like a cross between a California surfer boy and a computer nerd, and was paranoid to boot.

He stepped past her and kept going toward the stairs. "I'm Kate," she said. "I live downstairs. If you need anything—"

The upstairs door opened and then slammed shut.

3

OH, NO. Kate groaned when she saw the note taped to the washing machine. *Now what?*

"Occupant of Apartment B," the note was headed.

Plunking her overflowing laundry basket on the floor, Kate ripped the scrap of paper from under the tape. The sight of the cramped black scrawl annoyed her even before she read the note.

Occupant of Apartment B,
    Please don't leave your clothes in the washer.
    Thank you.
                    D. Edgar. (Occupant of Apartment A)

"Now, what's his problem?" Kate grumbled, her words echoing off the gray cement walls of the duplex's laundry room.

Glancing around, she quickly spotted the problem and uttered a cry of distress. On top of the dryer was a tangled, limp mess of pink and white. She recognized the remains of her brand new satin camisole, which had started life a sexy deep red. The camisole snaked around a pair of formerly white men's briefs that blushed furiously at the intimacy.

Just before breakfast she had carefully put the camisole on to wash in cold water and mild soap. Occupant

A had obviously thrown in his clothes without checking that the washer was empty and cranked up the hot water.

And goodbye to last month's clothing treat.

Kate held the limp, twisted fabric up to her body and sighed. The pitiful remains of the camisole hardly covered her full breasts. It had shrunk as well as run, ruined beyond hope.

Screwing the camisole into a ball, she hurled it at the trash. "Jerk," she muttered. Tossing back her hair, she poked her tongue at the ceiling, in the general direction of her brand-new upstairs neighbor.

Furiously she stuffed her laundry—bright reds, greens, blues, purples and dramatic blacks—into the washer and cranked the water setting back to cold. Should she stand here in the laundry room until her load was done? Computer brain might blow a circuit if he came in and discovered she'd started washing laundry and left it again.

Kate had known in her heart she wouldn't be lucky enough to get another Annie for a neighbor, but she had hoped for someone compatible.

What she'd got was the biggest jerk on the planet.

Now he was messing with her clothes. And, instead of apologizing, he was blaming her for his own mistake.

Picking up his blotchy pink briefs, she shook them at the ceiling.

"If you think I'm taking this, you need to learn a thing or two about Occupant of Apartment B."

She had to live here, but she didn't have to put up with a rude and unpleasant neighbor. Since he'd ignored her initial greeting, they hadn't seen each other again. She was working more hours than not, and he never seemed to leave his apartment.

The slammed door was bad enough, but no way she was putting up with snarky correspondence in the laundry room. But how should she send the man a message that she wasn't to be messed with?

A cold note like his wasn't going to have enough impact. Kate paused, still holding the formerly white discount-store briefs, and an idea hit her. She knew how to send him the message. A glance at her watch told her she had just enough time.

She was still smiling when she pushed through the doors of the department store and sailed toward Men's Wear. Shirts, ties, T-shirts, socks—her gaze roamed the aisles until she spotted what she was searching for.

As she entered the department, she felt uncomfortable. Did nice girls buy underwear for men they'd never met?

"Can I help you?" The young male voice stopped her in her tracks. Lunging toward a pile of woolen socks, Kate grabbed a pair of scratchy gray knee-highs and turned, pinning a bright smile on her face.

"No thanks, just looking around."

The clerk was a pimply faced boy, likely not out of his teens, and his eyes bulged when she faced him. His protuberant gaze reminded her how tight her fuchsia tank was—maybe she should have bought the large, after all—and how short her black skirt.

"Well." The word came out like a squeak. He flushed and tried again. "If you want anything, let me know. I'll be, like, you know...here."

Her own embarrassment evaporated in a smile.

"Thanks," she said casually, sifting through the socks until he moved away.

She slunk around, feeling as guilty as though she were planning to rob the place, until there was no sign of customer or clerk, then sidled into the racks of briefs, where she lost her embarrassment in the joy of the hunt.

Scanning the rows of possibilities, she was drawn first to a pair with a deep blue background dotted with perky sunshine-yellow happy faces.

No, she decided, too happy.

Then she almost succumbed to a pair of designer bikinis emblazoned with red-and-white hearts—one prominent red heart centered in the front—but heaven forbid the jerk should think she was coming on to him.

At last, she spotted them—a pair of deep burgundy bikinis adorned with ivory-colored Rubenesque cherubs. She chuckled aloud. They were more expensive than anything with so little fabric should be, but the delicious sense of revenge was worth it.

Disguising the briefs under a pair of the gray socks, Kate wandered surreptitiously out of Men's Wear and kept walking until she found a pay station with a female cashier.

She was running late for her shift by the time she returned home from the mall so she ran into the laundry room, propped the designer briefs on the dryer and penned a quick note:

Dear Occupant of Apartment A,

Tell your mother this is what men wear nowadays.

These are on me. (Crossed out).

These are for you.

Please look in washer before you add clothes next time.

K. Monahan (Occupant of Apartment B)

CURIOSITY TUGGED HER to the laundry room the next morning. A basket of clean towels was her cover, in case Occupant A happened to be there. She was dying to see whether or not he had picked up his new briefs.

They were gone. In their place on top of the dryer was a gold-and-white box embossed with the name of Seattle's most expensive lingerie shop.

Intrigued, Kate walked over to it. She didn't see a note. Putting down the basket of towels, she removed the cover from the box. Inside, even the gold-and-white tissue was printed with the store's name. Very classy. She breathed in the scent of roses emitted by the rustling tissue as she dug into the box.

A gleam of palest cream-colored silk peeked out. She stroked it softly before withdrawing an exquisite camisole embroidered with dainty peach rosettes. The tag told her what she had already guessed, the garment was pure silk. Even without a price sticker, Kate knew this camisole was far more costly than the red polyester satin it was replacing. The garment tag also told her it was the correct size.

How could Occupant A have guessed? She stood for a moment, horrified to think he'd checked out her body while blowing her off.

She stood frowning, caressing the soft silk thoughtfully until she remembered the discarded camisole in the trash can. Sure enough, when she picked it up she saw the size label had been neatly snipped off. He'd thought of everything. Maybe he was trying to say he was sorry? She rubbed the soft fabric against her cheek and then noticed the note in the box.

Dear Occupant of Apartment B,

This is what women of taste have always worn.

D. Edgar (Occupant of Apartment A)

Kate felt a sharp pang of hurt. *Women of taste.* How classy that sounded.

Women of taste didn't grow up in her neighborhood fighting with four other siblings for a few minutes in the bathroom in the morning. Women of taste had hours to bathe and scent themselves before stepping into their silk lingerie. Kate was probably the only one in her family who owned lingerie—even if it was only polyester.

And what did Occupant A know about women of taste? Him with his too-bright shirts and horrendous hair? In the week since he'd moved in, the only company he'd had was that computer of his.

Who did he think he was to insult her like this?

Kate had an Irish temper to match her auburn hair and green eyes, and it blazed into life in a sudden rage. A veil of red shimmered before her gaze as she snatched up the camisole and marched up the outside stairs.

She was banging on the door of Apartment A in no time, ready to explode. She could hardly stand still;

phrases she would say to him bubbled madly in her boiling anger.

The door opened.

Before Occupant A could say a word, Kate threw the silk camisole in his face.

It snagged on his glasses, hanging like a tassel on a life-size loser lamp.

"Who the hell do you think you are?" she shouted.

His eyes widened.

"How dare you..." she spluttered, looking at the badly dressed, slouching, bespectacled figure in front of her.

"How dare you—*you* suggest *I* don't have taste. When I need tips on how to dress from a surfer boy comic strip I'll ask you!"

He opened his mouth to speak but she kept on shouting.

"I happen to work in a beauty salon. It contains the word *beauty*, which is something you don't know the first thing about. I have plenty of taste and not...not...computer chips for brains."

"I—"

Kate drew a shuddering breath and raised her hand to shake her forefinger in his face. "Furthermore, I hate your attitude and your rude behavior and your stupid notes and I think you owe me an apology because—"

"You're right." The words were quiet and calm.

She'd expected a shouting match and the quiet words caught her off guard.

Occupant A had taken off his glasses in order to unsnag the camisole, which seemed to be caught in the hinge. He looked down, fiddling.

"What?" she shrieked.

A pair of clear gray eyes met hers ruefully. "I said, 'You're right.' I was out of line." He sighed, his face wrinkling as though in pain. "I apologize."

All Kate could think was what a shame it was that such beautiful eyes were wasted on a jerk who covered them up with glasses and stared at a computer monitor all day.

With a nod that sent her dangling earrings swinging, she said, "Well, okay. No more nasty notes."

"It was a stupid thing to do," he agreed.

His voice was a surprise. Deep and rich, with an upper-crust East Coast accent.

Kate drew a long breath. She'd expected a battle. Adrenaline pumped through her body. She'd been ready to rant and rave and throw things.

His unexpected apology took the wind out of her sails, leaving her stalled on his doorstep, with no anger to push her on. Her rages were always over as suddenly as they began, and in the calm aftermath she felt a little foolish. She backed up a couple of steps and, taking another shaky breath, suddenly smiled.

"I'm sorry, too, if my temper led me to say anything I shouldn't have."

When she smiled at him she noticed his eyes widen in shock and he shoved the now-freed glasses back on his face.

She turned to leave.

"Wait."

She glanced back.

He was holding out the camisole. "Please keep this."

"Oh, I couldn't. It's much too expensive." It occurred

to her that this man didn't know you could buy inexpensive camisoles at any department store, as she had. He must think you had to go to a lingerie store, or one of those fancy catalogs. "You could return it."

He straightened from his careless slouch and looked down at her. He was surprisingly tall when he stood upright, over six feet. "I'm not going to take it back. If you accept it I'll know you're not still mad at me."

Something in his voice, a trace of command, made her reach out to take the wisp of silk from him. "All right," she agreed softly. "It's beautiful. Thanks."

Feeling even more foolish, she turned once again to leave.

"Maybe we should set up a schedule?"

Puzzled, she turned back. "A schedule?"

"For the laundry. If each of us has assigned laundry days, we won't have a problem in future."

Kate thought of Annie and her in the laundry room together chatting, throwing their jeans and socks together to make up a load. It used to be so much fun. She sighed. "Sure."

"I'll put something together on my computer. Do you have a preference?"

"I don't know anything about computers."

He grinned. She was amazed to see he *could* grin. "I meant days of the week."

"Oh, of course. Well, I work different shifts. I'm busiest on the weekends and usually not so busy midweek."

"I can work with that." He cleared his throat. "Um." He seemed to be struggling. Finally he held out his hand. "My name's Dean Edgar."

"Kate Monahan." She grasped the outstretched hand, which clasped hers with warm strength. She glanced up in surprise.

He pulled his hand back as though she'd given him an electric shock. Then suddenly he was gone, back into his apartment like a gopher diving down into its burrow.

She shook her head as she walked slowly down the steps. He was a strange one, all right. But she didn't think she'd have any more trouble with him, now she'd let him know she was not to be messed with.

He was even kind of cute when you got past the hair and the wardrobe.

And there was that odd tug of familiarity. It was surprising, but she worked on a lot of men in the salon. He probably looked like one of her clients.

Not that any of her clients would ever leave her chair with their hair like that.

4

DARREN KNEW he'd been a fool the minute he opened the door and his sexy new neighbor started yelling at him.

He'd played his part so well, careful to make sure she wouldn't want anything to do with him—and doing it with notes had been a master stroke—because then she never got close enough to see him clearly.

He had to act like a jerk. He needed to keep his distance from everyone in his new life. Especially hot, sexy redheads who lived at the same address. Why couldn't he have had the luck to land in a building where his fellow tenant was another guy, or a married couple with kids? Anyone but a woman who made him remember how much he liked women.

When he'd received her sassy note and a pair of bikinis, he'd been furious. The part of him that was still Darren Edgar Kaiser Jr. had taken over his actions. The women Darren Kaiser knew didn't treat him like this. So he'd bought the most elegant camisole he could find and penned a note as insulting as hers had been.

The minute she'd launched the camisole at him, he knew he'd gone too far.

It was the look of angry hurt in her eyes that made him apologize. In wanting to be certain she left him alone he had never intended to hurt her feelings. Make her think he was a jerk? Yes. Make her question her own attractiveness? No.

He'd glimpsed her through the window a few times. The way she strutted in her flamboyant clothing, she certainly didn't look like a woman who was insecure about her appearance.

So he'd acted out of character. The Dean Edgar character he and Bart had invented would never have apologized.

Of course, Dean Edgar would never buy a camisole like that in the first place. Then he certainly wouldn't have stood there while his gorgeous neighbor yelled at him—picturing the soft silk against Kate's creamy skin and auburn hair, imagining those pink cheeks flushed, not with anger, but with passion....

He'd been a fool, all right.

Darren stomped back to his computer, stretching his cramped shoulders. He removed the heavy glasses, rubbing absently at the indentation they left on the bridge of his nose, and sat down to get back to work. One thing he'd proved was that his disguise was working. Kate hadn't treated him as though he were America's most eligible bachelor; she'd looked as if she felt sorry for him.

The one good thing about the magazine disaster was that it had allowed him to leave the family firm and try to make his own career. This was the silver lining inside the black cloud of notoriety. All he needed to finish his software program was a few months with no distractions.

His mind wandered to the scene at his front door.

Kate.

Under the general heading *Distractions*, Kate would top the list.

She'd been so angry with him she couldn't get the words out fast enough. Even her hair got angry, bouncing and swinging as she shouted at him, shooting fire every time the sun hit it. That hair curled all the way down her back.

It was amazing.

The stuff of fantasies.

Still, he reasoned, if she worked at a beauty salon it could be fake.

Yeah. That should stop any fantasies before they started. Every time he thought about that hair, he would imagine her taking it off before she went to bed. And he would do the same thing with the camisole.

No!

He just wouldn't think about the camisole at all.

The blinking cursor on his screen reminded him that he'd been daydreaming again. He swore. He wondered how Kate would have reacted if she'd known who he really was. A reluctant grin pulled at his mouth. He had a strong feeling she wouldn't care a bit whom she was yelling at once she lost her temper.

Darren dragged his concentration back to the computer once more, but words and images danced meaninglessly on the screen.

He started typing.

He stopped.

He breathed deeply.

Kate was taking off her hair before she went to bed.

Underneath it—let's see—she'd gone prematurely gray and had her own hair in a crew cut.

And he was not thinking about the camisole at all.

"SMELLS FANTASTIC," Kate's co-worker and best friend, Ruby, was over for dinner, a tradition they'd started that allowed them to visit inexpensively outside of salon hours.

She affected a bad imitation of a broad Irish brogue. "And you'll be makin' some lucky man a fine little wife."

"Thank you, Ma," Kate replied in a more authentic brogue. "But don't be marryin' me off now, till you've tasted it."

"Here's to mothers." Ruby raised her glass in a toast. "How is your mom, anyway?"

"Oh, I don't know. The same. They're all the same."

"Susan and her crew moved out yet?"

She shook her head. Susan, the eldest of the five children, was the only married one, and the only child apart from Kate who'd left home. She'd been married four years and had two children, but when her husband lost his job the four of them had moved back in with her mother and her other siblings. The small two-bedroom bungalow Kate grew up in now housed eight of her family.

"And I thought I'd lived in tenements." Ruby shook her head.

"You did live in tenements. You're just not Irish."

The aromatic scent of lasagna filled the air as she scooped hefty portions onto two plates. A basket of crusty garlic bread and a big bowl of salad lay between the two women.

"Oh, I wish I could cook," wailed Ruby as she did every time she came to Kate's for dinner. "Will you marry me?"

Kate shook her head. "I'm looking for somebody with enough money to get me out of hairdressing."

"Well, that lets me out. What about that escaped bachelor fellow I keep hearing about on the news? Maybe you could find him and pick up the reward."

Kate snorted. "I never even find my lost earrings." She vaguely recalled the blond man on the front of Bethany's magazine. "I'm not sure I'm the type rich men go for."

"I hear you. Why do people with money always look for people with more money? You'd think they'd try and spread the wealth a little. It's more democratic."

"I don't know. But I do know that you have to rely on yourself. Dreaming of rich guys doesn't help."

"What about your bank man? He looks like a guy with money to spend."

"You mean Brian."

"Yeah, right. How's it going?"

Kate sipped wine, thinking. "He's been working really hard lately and so have I, so we haven't seen each other that much."

"Looked to me last time I saw him like he was getting set to propose. You going to marry him?"

Kate broke apart a piece of garlic bread, the crust crunching in the silence. "No. I can't explain it. Sure, he's good-looking and has a great job, but I'm pretty sure he wants kids right away." Suddenly a bubble of despair welled up inside her. "Oh, Ruby, I'm just so tired of looking after people."

Across the table Ruby's chocolate eyes were soft with sympathy. "Don't I know it."

When the two had met at the beauty salon, they'd become instant friends. As they got to know each other, it was uncanny how similar their backgrounds were. Both came from big families headed by single women: Ruby's through divorce, Kate's through her father's death. She'd quit high school to help her mother out financially, and to look after the younger kids since her mom had to get a job long before her grief had healed. A big chunk of both her and Ruby's paychecks still went straight home to their mothers even though they had moved out on their own.

Both were willing to make extra sacrifices not to live at home ever again. Living alone meant working extra shifts, skipping breaks to squeeze a few more customers into each day, eating a lot of macaroni and being very creative with little clothing. They both agreed their freedom and the luxury of privacy was worth any sacrifice.

"He doesn't know about your family, does he?" Ruby asked.

"No." Brian certainly didn't know that her mother relied on Kate's financial support. And he didn't strike Kate as the kind of man who would ever take on that burden himself once they were married. If she did marry him, how could she give her mother money and keep it a secret?

"Well, don't rush into anything," was Ruby's advice, which was pretty much what Kate had already decided.

"Yes. We're sort of taking a break from each other for

a little while. It's easier than both of us having to cancel plans because we're working overtime." She rose to clear the table and paused. "Plus, I think the spark's gone. You know?"

After dinner, they moved to sit on the couch. Ruby unscrewed the cap on the bottle and topped up their glasses. "So, heard anything more from Angel-Butt?" she asked. Having heard the whole story, she'd now christened Kate's upstairs neighbor with that nickname.

Nodding mysteriously, Kate rose from the table and crossed to the adjacent bedroom, returning with the gold-and-white box. Ruby let out a low whistle when she saw the name of the shop. Her jaw dropped when she removed the camisole, touching it reverently. "Oh, honey! This is to die for. Was there a note?" she asked.

Kate recited it.

Ruby laughed. "Revenge of the Nerd?"

She told her friend about storming up to his apartment, and his apology, while Ruby continued fondling the silk camisole.

"And he can afford this?"

"I guess so. I told him to take it back, but he insisted I keep it, just to show there's no hard feelings."

"He's got good taste for a nerd." Ruby let out a lusty chuckle. "Why, you should model this for him some night." Ruby thrust out her impressive chest and held the camisole against it. "Give that angel a workout."

THE QUIET TAP OF THE computer keys was the only sound in the room, but Darren was having trouble concentrating. He was hungry, and he was spending so many hours alone he was starting to worry about his mental health.

Sure, he wanted to work on his project, and yes, if the media got hold of him there'd be hell to pay, but still he needed to get out more.

Little noises from downstairs told him his neighbor was home. And that was his biggest problem. The person in Seattle he most wanted to socialize with—the only one he knew—was the one he most needed to stay away from.

He told himself it was simply loneliness and not his frustrated libido that had him thinking about her when he ought to be working. Thinking about her reminded him of the schedule that anal-retentive Dean Edgar had promised to draft.

He worked out a very Dean Edgarish schedule, coded in blocks, that gave him exclusive use of the laundry facilities Saturday, Sunday and Wednesday, while Kate got Monday, Tuesday, Thursday and Friday. He printed the schedule and was just about to take it to her when he heard shrieks of laughter coming from the downstairs apartment. He smiled, enjoying the sound. Kate must have a friend over, and something had struck them pretty funny.

The laughter downstairs emphasized how quiet it was in his apartment. His first Saturday night in Seattle and he was sitting here all alone, not knowing a soul in the city and dressed like a goof. He shook his head.

Was he crazy?

He thought back to what he would be doing back home on a Saturday night. He almost groaned at the thought of all he'd left behind—the restaurants, the parties, the clubs, the women.

He glanced out the window. The stars were out tonight. Maybe he'd take a walk by himself and go find something to eat in a restaurant where there were other people. He gazed down at the quiet tree-lined street.

A young black woman emerged from the downstairs apartment, throwing a laughing comment over her shoulder. He heard Kate's voice calling out in reply. Great, the friend was gone, he could drop the schedule off on his way out.

He donned the glasses and an old jeans jacket Bart and he had found in a thrift store, shoved a Mariners cap on his head and let himself out of his apartment, the computer printout in his hand. He ran lightly down the stairs and knocked on Kate's door.

"Honestly, Ruby, you always forget something." Kate was laughing as she opened the door. The smile turned to an O of surprise when she saw Darren standing there. For some reason she blushed when she saw him.

"Hi," he said.

"Hi," she answered, an embarrassed smile playing around her lips. She had bright yellow rubber gloves on, drops of soapy water clinging to them. They looked like clown hands, Darren thought, incongruous against the cherry-red sleeveless cotton sweater and jeans. Instead of shoes she wore oversize gray wool socks.

He cleared his throat. "I brought you the schedule," he said, trying to hand it to her, but she backed away, laughing and flapping her wet yellow gloves.

"My hands are all wet. You'd better come in."

Stepping into her apartment, he was assailed by delicious aromas: garlic and cheese, spicy tomato sauce. He breathed in rapturously. "Smells like a little Italian restaurant I used to love on..." He stopped himself before he mentioned East Seventy-third street. What was the matter with him? His cover was slipping again. "I can't remember where it was," he finished lamely. She didn't look too surprised. She already thought he was a lame sort of guy.

"Lasagna." She smiled. "You probably haven't had time to get organized, do you want some?"

"No thanks," he said, before his stomach and every other part of him could make him say yes.

She was even prettier when she wasn't yelling. Her eyes were big and green with flecks of gold. Her lips were full and kissable. And that hair—if it was real— would be glorious to touch.

She peeled off the gloves and took the schedule from him. "Sure, this looks fine," she said, casually perusing the page, then she focused intently. "You remembered my first and last name. And spelled it right, too." She looked at him curiously. "Are you Irish?"

He chuckled, unable to resist. "No, I've got computer chips for brains, remember?" He leaned against the doorjamb, casually, watching one particular ringlet brush her temple. He could have watched it for hours. He'd never seen anyone with such sexy hair.

She put her hand to her cheek. She had the kind of fair skin that blushed easily. "Did I say that to you?"

"Among other things." The urge to indulge in a little light banter, initiate the game, was strong. It took an effort of will to prevent himself, to move away from the wall and stoop as he backed outside.

"I'll post that schedule in the laundry room, then. If there's anything else we should schedule, like lawn mowing, or garbage duty or whatever, just let me know." His glasses were sliding down his nose; he jabbed them irritably back up with a forefinger.

"Okay," she said, a hint of humor in her voice. "'Night."

"'Night."

A long walk would do him good. He needed something to get his mind off the first attractive female he'd met in Seattle.

It was a clear night. From the duplex on Queen Anne Hill, Darren sauntered downhill in the general direction of the harbor. The smell of summer was in the air, assorted flowers, freshly mown grass and dogwood trees in full bloom.

After a good long walk, he'd worked up quite an appetite. He passed through Pioneer Square, his feet stumbling over the restored cobbled roads. He liked this area of town. Many of the late nineteenth-century buildings had been preserved and the old shells housed new life: coffee bars, offices, shops and restaurants.

He saw bright light spilling out of a corner pub and his stomach grumbled audibly. He read the name lettered on the door—O'Malley's. He smiled to himself. It was a night for the Irish.

Inside, the atmosphere was warm. Wood paneling and a massive bar that must have been as old as the building gave an antique charm to the place. Taking a seat near the end of the long bar, Darren ordered a Redhook ale, brewed locally he was assured, and a burger. Remembering to slouch was no problem as he tried to perch his tall frame on a bar stool.

A couple of attractive women came in and looked around for somewhere to sit. They looked him over and then sat at the other end of the bar. He'd never thought of himself as attractive to women, because he'd just never thought about it. But being evaluated and found lacking was a new and unpleasant experience.

As the bar filled up, no one but the bartender came near him.

He was just finishing his second beer and thinking about heading home when a slight, balding man entered O'Malley's. His cheap suit hung awkwardly on his bony frame. The light seemed to bother him, or maybe it was a tic that caused him to blink rapidly as he looked around the room. Darren chuckled silently when the man chose the stool next to him. It seemed the man saw in him a kindred spirit. If he had to strike up a conversation with a stranger, he wished it had been the pretty girls.

The man ordered a cheeseburger and a light beer. He took a sip of his drink and turned to Darren. "Nice evening," he said.

"Yeah."

The man squinted and blinked a few times. "I wish I had my glasses on. Darn contact lenses are driving me crazy. I only wear them when I see clients."

"What kind of work do you do?" Darren asked politely, waiting to be bored.

"Computer programming."

His boredom disappeared. "No kidding, that's my line of work."

The two were soon deep in conversation, engaged in the instant bonding of two people who share the same passion. Finally, the man introduced himself as Harvey Shield. He said, "I'm surprised we haven't met before. Who do you work for?"

"I just moved to Seattle."

The blinking eyes surveyed him sharply for a few moments. Taking another sip of beer, he said, "You seem pretty knowledgeable, where'd you go to school?"

"MIT."

"Ever have a Professor Elliot?"

"Old Nellie? Sure. He was a mean old boot, but he sure knew operating systems."

Harvey Shield nodded. "Had a habit of failing more students than he passed." He took another drink of his beer. "How'd you do?"

Darren returned the scrutiny. The man beside him had contacts in the computer industry. Now was not the time for false modesty. He grinned. "Top of the class."

Harvey grinned back. "So was I, fifteen years ago." He sighed, as though a weight had been lifted off his shoulders. "Listen, I need another programmer on my team. We're falling behind on a big job. I don't have time for ads in the paper and interviews. How'd you like to come work for us for a while on contract?"

Darren blinked. He hadn't intended to look for a job, but one week of spending 24/7 with only a computer for company had him convinced that a longer stint of that was not healthy. Besides, with no other distractions, he thought about his downstairs neighbor far too often. A job in his industry would get him out of the house, give him other like-minded types to connect with, and the extra money meant he could stay in Seattle as long as he needed. He already had his own company set up, with a separate tax ID, so his paychecks wouldn't even have his name on them.

He was very glad he'd chosen this particular night, and this particular bar. "Harvey," he said extending his hand, "you have yourself a deal."

Darren walked back home in an entirely different mood. He had a job. Dean Edgar had snagged it all on his own without any help from the Kaiser name. And he had freedom like he'd never had in his life with months stretching ahead to work on his project. To succeed or fail on his own terms.

He was whistling softly when he got back to the duplex. He had to pass Kate's door to get to the stairway that led up to his own apartment. She had a motion-sensitive light hooked up that almost blinded him when it shone full on his glasses.

As he dropped his head in reaction, he had the unpleasant but now familiar experience of seeing his own newsprint-grainy face grinning up from the bottom of the recycling bin.

With a muttered curse he leaned down and snatched the paper up. Please, let them not have figured out he was in Seattle.

"Can't afford your own copy?" He jumped at the sound of Kate's voice from behind him. She sounded half amused, half exasperated.

Fighting the urge to hide the wretched thing behind his back, he flipped the paper inside out to hide his picture. "Sorry, I...ah...forgot to buy today's. Just wanted to check the sports scores."

The shock of seeing himself in the *Seattle-Post Intelligencer* made him unusually clumsy and suddenly a cascade of newsprint hit the ground. His grinning face mocked him from dead center. He stomped his sneaker square on his own face, and squatted, grabbing what he could and scrunching the paper back in the recycling bin.

Kate dropped down beside him. "Here's the Lifestyle section." She looked up at him and with a shake of her head thrust the section back in the bin. She picked up another bundle, and he could see she'd retrieved the fashion page. She didn't say a word, just gave a secret little smile and shoved it on top of the Lifestyle section.

"It's okay. I can manage," He sounded desperate. He *felt* desperate; pretty soon he was going to have to move his foot.

She was so close, her hair kept swinging against his shoulder, gleaming chestnut and ruby when she moved. No wonder she worked in a beauty salon, she was a walking advertisement for her profession. She even smelled like a beauty salon: like tropical fruit and exotic lotions. How was he supposed to think straight?

The best strategy he could come up with to prevent her from seeing the picture in the paper was to turn his head and kiss that smug smile off her red lips.

Desperate times call for desperate measures. He turned his head, longing quite fiercely to kiss her, even though it would earn him a well-deserved slap at the very least.

She turned her head at the same time, smiled and held up a page.

"Sports scores," she announced gaily.

Using the sports section as a shield, he quickly tossed the rest of the pages, including the one with his picture, into the blue bin.

He fled upstairs with a bunch of unwanted sports scores and an ache of longing in his chest.

He wished he'd had an excuse to kiss her.

Once he was back in his own apartment, he flipped on the television to catch some news before he went to bed. There was news, all right. Lots of news. The usual trouble in hot spots, the murders, the strikes, the endless politics. And then the soft features. After seeing his face on the front of Kate's paper, it didn't entirely surprise him to see himself on the TV, but it was still a nasty shock.

Damn it, why couldn't they leave him alone?

The story was simple. *Matchmaker* magazine's Match of the Year was missing. Yes, indeedy. His bolt from the metropolis had not gone unnoticed. He scowled at his TV. Was every news outlet in America this hard up for news or was this whole thing some cosmic joke engineered by God, or more likely Darren's father, to destroy Darren Jr.'s chance to prove himself in his own way.

Balked at finding their prey, eligible bachelor-hunting women were going public to find Darren and convince him to return home to various promised treats ranging from dirty weekends to love everlasting.

Serena Ashcroft was one damn smart operator, Darren realized with a sour smirk. He'd disappeared in order to lessen his news value. She'd turned his disappearance *into* news. Now the chase was on to find the missing Match of the Year. The magazine was posting a reward—and he couldn't help but wonder if dear old dad hadn't kicked in a few bucks—which immediately made him feel churlish.

His dad had been loudly angry, but he'd never betray his son intentionally.

Women were appealing for help in locating him. He might as well be on *America's Most Wanted*.

His only consolation was that he'd been sighted more often than Elvis recently, everywhere from Noma, Alaska, to Baton Rouge, Louisiana. People were calling in from all over who'd swear they'd seen him walking down the street, eating in a restaurant, buying gas. No one knew he was in Seattle. He was going to work in what sounded like a small, unpretentious computer firm, and when he wasn't working, he was going to be hiding out here at home working on his own projects.

So long as his sexy neighbor didn't clue in to his identity, he felt as well-hidden here as anywhere.

5

DARREN YANKED OFF his glasses and rubbed his tired eyes. He was having trouble focusing on the computer screen. He'd need real glasses soon. Two weeks at his cozy little job with SYX Systems to give him a few hours out of the house was more like a nightmare you could never wake from. Harvey hadn't been kidding when he'd said they were behind on a big job.

Darren didn't see how they were going to meet the deadline, even with all of them working eighteen-hour shifts. His dad—who'd wanted him to take over the advertising firm and not waste his time on computers—would be thrilled if he could see how much Darren was beginning to hate the sight of a computer screen.

The most frustrating part of his job at SYX was that it left him little time or energy to work on his own programs. Darren had fully intended to work eighteen-hour days once he started working for Harvey, but he'd planned on spending nine each day at work and another nine on his own project. If the pace didn't let up, he'd have to quit. Except he hated quitting a job before it was done; he liked the people he worked with; he was getting out of his apartment regularly; and, best of all, he doubted anyone here had ever heard of *Matchmaker*. Reward hunters, women with love on their minds and reporters could comb Seattle and the chances were good they'd never find him.

He heard a droning monotone that indicated Harvey was rallying the troops. As a motivator, the man was no fireball.

Harvey came weaving among the workstations toward Darren, buzzing and blinking like a fly caught in a beer bottle. He'd had to meet with the client again today, so he'd traded in his usual glasses, with lenses so thick he resembled a space creature, for the hated contact lenses.

"Tracked that bug down yet, Dean?" It had taken a while, but Darren was finally getting used to answering to Dean.

"Standing right in front of me." Darren mimicked a can of insect spray. "Pssst....pssst." He sprayed Harvey with the imaginary lethal aerosol.

His boss blinked, looking worried. "I meant the bug in the program."

The man had no sense of humor. Darren sighed and shoved his glasses back on. "Yeah, Harvey. I think I've disarmed it. I just need to test my fix."

In two weeks he'd become Harvey's right hand. They shared the obsession. Computers were more than just a job, they were magical creatures of endless fascination. If there were a Computer Addicts Anonymous, he and Harvey would be working on a twelve-step program.

"Just for today, I will not turn on my computer," Darren intoned gravely, "I will not touch it, communicate with it, worship its circuit boards." He didn't realize he was mumbling aloud until he saw Harvey's anxious face through the fog of tiredness.

"Maybe you should go home early." His boss appeared distinctly alarmed.

"But the night is young. It can't be more than nine or nine-thirty." In two weeks Darren hadn't once left before midnight.

Joseph Goode's voice joined the discussion. "It's nine-forty-five, and if you guys aren't fried, the rest of us are." Joseph was the only one of the computer programmers in the unit who was married, as he rarely let them forget. He swore his wife would think he was having an affair if he had to tell her he was working late every night.

Looking at him, Darren had a hard time believing he'd found *one* woman who could love him, never mind two. Apart from his annoying personality, there was the small problem of body odor.

Harvey looked around at the group of eight programmers, all bleary eyed and morose from lack of sleep. He blinked a few times and then nodded suddenly. "We'll knock off now. Yes. Good idea, Joseph. See you all back here first thing in the morning."

Darren drove home with the windows wide open to make sure he stayed awake. He was shivering when he finally stumbled out of the car. If he could just make it up the stairs, he could fall into bed and forget about computer bugs for a few hours.

He opened the door of his apartment and for a stunned moment thought he'd been burgled. He liked to keep his things tidy, and what he saw horrified him.

Dirty laundry was strewn all over the place—every night for two weeks, he'd stripped, discarding his clothes carelessly, and dropped into bed, so tired, he found it an effort to brush his teeth.

If he didn't watch it he'd be the next Joseph Goode. Sniffing the air gingerly, he thought he caught a whiff of old Joseph.

God, he stank.

He was wearing the same shirt he'd worn yesterday, because he'd discovered this morning he was out of clean clothes.

Laundry. That was it. He'd have to do some laundry. If he wasn't a grown man he would have cried. He was too tired to do laundry.

Stumbling like a drunk, he picked up jeans, socks that made his eyes water, shirts and underwear. He stripped, adding the discarded clothing to the pile, and threw the lot into the empty computer box that was his makeshift laundry hamper.

He shuffled into his bathrobe, shoved his feet into sneakers and slipped outside. The breeze of a summer evening reminded him forcibly that he was naked under his knee-length navy robe. He forced his tired legs to move faster into the laundry room next door to Kate's suite.

Darren stuffed the washer, added detergent and started the machine. He decided to wait for the load to finish so he could put his clothes in the dryer and a second load in the washer—no sense going upstairs, he'd just fall asleep and have nothing dry to wear tomorrow.

He'd never noticed how soothing the sound of a washing machine was. Maybe if he just rested his head on it for a minute...

"Dean...*Dean!*" Something was shaking him. Must be

Harvey. "Bugs all gone. Pssst pssst." He motioned his imaginary spray can at Harvey. "All fixed. Go away."

"Dean, wake up!"

That wasn't Harvey's voice. It was sweet, and lush and feminine. He was dreaming. That redhead downstairs was getting into his dreams again.

"Don't think about her," he ordered himself. "She's taking her hair off. Anybody can see it's fake," he mumbled. "No camisole. Not thinking about the camisole." Not thinking about the camisole made him smile. He was still smiling when the shaking finally woke him.

The woman from downstairs wasn't a dream, she was real and trying to pull him off the washing machine.

Darren raised his head slowly, attempting to focus on the woman in front of him.

One look at him and her eyes narrowed. She sniffed the air suspiciously, with her hands on her glorious, curvy hips. She'd pulled some of her curls on top of her head with a kind of elastic thing and they spilled down to join the rest, like a fountain.

"Have you been partying?" she demanded.

He shook his head to clear it. Walked over to the laundry sink and doused his face with cold water. "Mmm, sorry," he answered at last. "Not partying. Working."

"I was beginning to think you'd moved out." She still looked suspicious, but there was a hint of a smile in her big green eyes. She was wearing black pants that clung where they touched and a shiny lime-green shirt. She wore big gold hoops in her ears, more bright gold at her neck and bangles on her wrists.

"No, I got a job. The company's fallen behind on a big project, and we're working around the clock to catch up."

She seemed torn between amusement and annoyance. Then he saw the laundry basket on the floor beside her.

A horrible realization dawned. He groaned. "What day is it?"

It was definitely amusement in her eyes. "Tuesday. One of us seems to have misread the computer-generated schedule. Now, let's see..." She made a big production out of studying the schedule, running a bright red fingernail down the printout taped to the wall. "Why, I believe Tuesday is *my* day."

"I'm really sorry." He felt like a jackass. "It's just that I haven't had any time off in the last two weeks. I don't even know what day it is."

"That's okay, I hate schedules, anyway." Kate smiled widely, enjoying her triumph.

He just stood there, feeling too stupid from sleep deprivation to reply.

She looked at him for a long moment, and the amusement he read on her face changed to sympathy. "You look awfully tired, why don't you go to bed? I'll put your stuff in the dryer."

"Are you sure you don't mind?" He would argue if he wasn't so damned tired, but the idea of going to bed was too sweet to resist. And if he didn't go soon, he'd make a complete fool of himself by inviting her to go with him.

"Not at all. I usually do laundry on Tuesdays, anyway," she said sweetly.

He gave a tired chuckle. "Thanks, I owe you."

"Oh, and Dean?"

"Mmm?"

"You have nice legs, for a guy."

He'd forgotten he was wearing his robe. Exhausted or not, he left the laundry room at a trot, the bathrobe flapping with each hurried step.

Her bubbling laughter followed him all the way to his front door.

As she folded Dean's clothes, Kate shook her head over some of his choices. She couldn't make him out. He was so garish about his wardrobe and yet so reticent about normal friendliness. He was a mass of contradictions.

He must be awfully smart, though, to do all that complicated computer stuff. And when she'd caught him asleep on the washer, with his face unguarded, she'd felt an odd instinct to touch him. Nothing too drastic— she'd merely wanted to cup his cheek in her hand, or stroke his hair, the way you would with someone you felt affection for, which was a little crazy. She would never be attracted to someone like Dean. She was probably a little overtired, too.

Still, she stayed up longer than she'd intended to make sure his washing, as well as hers, was all done.

It seemed only moments later that the blaring alarm clock told Darren it was six-thirty. Stumbling out of bed, he made straight for the shower. It was only as he was toweling himself dry that he realized every piece of clothing Dean Edgar owned was in the laundry room. It took all his courage to don the bathrobe and prepare to walk past Kate's apartment to retrieve his clothes.

He never got past his front door.

On the landing outside, neatly folded, was his washing. She had even ironed his shirts. And she hadn't done it for Darren Kaiser Jr., heir to Kaiser Image Makers, or because some stupid magazine thought he was the Match of the Year, she'd done it for Dean Edgar, the geek with computer chips for brains.

He whistled as he dressed.

And was still whistling when he arrived at work in a freshly ironed shirt. As soon as the stores were open for the day, he called a florist and ordered a dozen long-stemmed pink roses to be delivered to Kate.

"Certainly, sir," the perky female voice said. "May I have your credit card number?"

His teeth ground audibly. *Fool.* Why did Kate Monahan make him act like he was Darren Kaiser again? All he needed was for some florist's clerk to tip off the media that Darren Edgar Kaiser Jr.'s credit card had just been used in Seattle. No. He was a cash only man these days.

"I'm sorry," he managed to say, coughing to disguise his voice. "I've changed my mind."

He put down the phone, resisting the urge to bang himself senseless with the receiver. Dean Edgar didn't send women long-stemmed roses by the dozen.

Okay, so what *did* Dean Edgar do? He decided on a little research. His colleagues were all versions of Dean Edgar. They would guide him.

He wandered back to his workstation. "Gord," he

called to a gangly young man with pale red hair and freckles who was probably the closest to himself in age.

"Whah?" Gord turned eyes so pale a blue they were almost colorless toward Darren.

"Gord, if a woman did you a favor and you wanted to thank her, what would you do?"

Gord scratched his neck. "You mean like give you a ride to work? Or make you dinner, something like that?"

"Yeah."

Gord looked up at the ceiling as though for inspiration. "I don't know, send her a thank-you e-mail, I guess," he finally answered.

There was no such thing as a private conversation among the programmers, they were jammed too tightly. Joseph Goode piped up. "You can't just send an e-mail, Gord. If a woman did something nice for me— I'm speaking hypothetically, of course, being a married man—I would buy her a small bottle of perfume. Ladies love perfume, you know," he announced in his smug way.

"Yeah, to drown out the smell of you, Sir Stinkalot," another programmer, Steve Adams, muttered.

Steve was less of an ubergeek than most of Harvey's hires, so Darren asked him, next.

"I'll tell you what you do, Dean." He leaned back as though contemplating the origins of the universe. "You want one of those big boxes of candy, in a red box—you know the ones? In the shape of a heart? You'll be in there before you know it." He made an obscene gesture in case Darren had any doubt what he meant by "in there."

"Great, thanks," Darren managed to say.

His other consultants suggested a fish fresh from Pike Place Market, a computer game, more candy and a gift certificate to a computer store.

Harvey suggested he stop wasting everybody's time since neither he nor anybody else had time for the ladies until the project was completed.

Darren decided he could please his two selves by going to Pike Place and buying fresh flowers. Ignoring Harvey's protests, he left the office.

He'd almost forgotten what daylight looked like.

He strolled down to the market, enjoying simply being out in the fresh air. He paused to enjoy the lively banter at the fish stall. He smelled all the smells—the seaweedy scent of the harbor, just-baked breads and pastries, coffee, spices and cheeses. His senses seemed starved after so many hours in front of a computer, and he let them all feast.

At the flower stall he hesitated over the colorful bouquets. None seemed quite right. Then a shelf of potted plants caught his eye. He remembered the jungle in Kate's living room, the pots of herbs growing on her window sill. He settled on a small hot pepper tree, then reluctantly he returned to work.

It was just after 1:00 a.m. when Darren got home. Taking the carefully wrapped plant out of the car, he stopped to scrawl a note that simply read *Thanks, Dean,* and set the plant by her front door before he dragged himself up to his apartment.

He didn't see Kate again until Sunday, when Harvey finally allowed the programmers a day off. Darren slept until early afternoon and woke feeling like his old self.

After cooking an omelet and tidying his apartment, he felt desperate for some fresh air and exercise. Digging out a pair of shorts and decent athletic shoes, he grabbed a faded blue T-shirt, made sure he had dark glasses and a ball cap pulled low over his face, and headed out for a run.

He fell into a blissful pounding rhythm, enjoying the warm air filling his lungs and the stretching and bunching of muscles that hadn't been exercised in weeks. He was streaming with sweat as he rounded the corner to his own street. He slowed to a walk, hunching his shoulders as soon as he saw Kate unloading groceries from her tiny hatchback.

She wore short shorts and a top that showed a lot of lightly tanned back. And the contours as she bent forward made his hands twitch. If anything, he was panting harder than during his run. Even after cursing himself for a pervert, he stood watching her bend over, digging around in the back of her car for something.

She was so different from any woman he'd known. Full of life in a sassy kind of way. He was used to cool elegance—they seemed to teach it in high school back where he came from. But what Kate had was a zesty flamboyance.

That and a body engineered for high performance.

He watched her pull up, a rogue apple in her hands, which she stuffed back into a grocery sack. She'd turn and spot him lusting after her body any minute.

"Need a hand?" he called out, stepping nearer.

She looked up and made a face. "No, thanks, you might drip on something."

He waved and carried on up to his place.

She raised her voice behind him. "Hey, I'm making a chicken stir-fry for dinner so I can try out my new hot peppers. Want to come down and eat with me?"

"Love to," he called back before he could stop himself. "I'll bring the wine."

The pleasure of an evening in with a beautiful sexy woman was one he hadn't enjoyed in a while. And this particular sexy, beautiful woman was someone he needed to keep his distance from if he wanted the Match of the Year's whereabouts to remain a mystery. He really shouldn't tempt himself—or fate.

He also knew he'd spend the rest of the day counting the minutes until he could see her again.

6

KATE WAS JUST putting the second earring in her ear when the knock came. They were flea-market earrings of brass and iridescent beads that livened up her short denim skirt and white sleeveless blouse.

She opened the door to her upstairs neighbor and was vaguely disappointed to see him in the thick glasses. Twice now she'd seen him without them and she liked his eyes. They were honest, direct eyes. It was harder to see them through the thick lenses.

He'd obviously dressed for the occasion in one of the more flamboyant of his shirts. And that was saying something. It was green and had some sort of jungle-vine motif and she thought those splashes of color might be representative of tropical birds. Or the designer's drug-induced hallucination. Hard to tell, really.

Kate flashed Dean a friendly smile as she took the proffered bottle inside its brown bag and put it on the kitchen counter.

"Thanks. Come on in." She led him through the living room and out to the back patio.

"This is nice," he said, glancing around at the potted geraniums and the plastic Adirondack chairs and patio table she'd picked up on sale at the end of summer last year.

"Thanks. Your place is a lot bigger than mine, but I really like the patio. Look around. I'll finish dinner."

She walked back into the kitchen and found Dean had followed her. "What can I do to help?" he asked.

The rice was done, the chicken was perfect, the colorful array of vegetables just about crisp tender. Pulling out her all-purpose pasta bowl ready to receive the meal, she noticed the wine still on the counter.

"You can open the wine."

"No problem." He pulled the bottle out of the bag, and her eyes widened at the elegant label.

"Oh—oh," she said. "On my budget I only drink screw-top wines. I don't even own a corkscrew." She bit her lip. "Do you have one upstairs?"

"Even better." With a flourish he produced from his pocket the biggest Swiss Army knife she'd ever seen. He pulled out a pair of scissors, tweezers, and a knife that looked sharp enough for brain surgery before he found the corkscrew. He must have interpreted her look correctly for he nodded. "I was a model Boy Scout."

"Why am I not surprised?"

She took everything outside and he followed with the wine and a couple of glasses, then waited until she was seated before sitting down himself. Such manners...

She had wondered if he would be a difficult guest, but he had picked up some social graces somewhere, and conversation was surprisingly easy.

"Mmm," he said, munching happily. "You would not believe how happy I am to be eating real food. I've lived off takeout and fast food for the last three weeks."

"I'm glad you like it," Kate answered. "To be honest

with you, I love to cook, and I don't have much opportunity living alone."

"No boyfriend?" he asked in surprise, then shook his head sharply. "Sorry. None of my business."

She wrinkled her nose. There was something about Dean that made it easy for her to confide in him. For one thing, he didn't know any of her friends. Well, he didn't know a soul in Seattle, so even if he blabbed all her secrets, they wouldn't get around. And he didn't seem like the type to blab, anyway. Plus, he was—she didn't know exactly. Comfortable, somehow.

"We're sort of taking a break," she said.

Her companion just nodded, leaving it up to her whether she wanted to continue the conversation.

"I'm..." She sighed and twisted the stem of her glass around in her fingers.

"What?"

"Have you ever felt you were getting pushed in a certain direction and you weren't sure you wanted to go there?"

"Oh, have I ever," he said with such feeling she blinked. "But this is about you. Go on."

"It's hard to explain. He works for a bank, has a good steady job with a great future. He's nice, good-looking, fun to be with." When she listed Brian's good qualities, she wondered why they were taking a break. Then she remembered. "But I think he wants to get serious, and I'm not sure."

"Serious. You mean move-in-together serious?"

She laughed. "I'm Irish Catholic, Dean. My mother would kill me before she'd see me live in sin. No. I mean marriage serious."

"Wow."

"Yes. I feel like it's all moving too fast. I think he wants kids right away."

Dean blinked at her. "Kids right away? Is he in some kind of a race?"

She laughed. "No. He's just...ambitious, I suppose." But hearing a stranger's take on this made her wonder. Brian did seem to be in a big hurry to get to a place most people took years to reach. Her instincts were telling her to take things easy. And the longer she and Brian were apart, the less likely it seemed they'd ever end up together. Soon, she was going to have to make a decision.

"And you don't want kids?"

"I do." She glanced up, surprised she was telling him all this, and yet feeling instinctively she could trust him. "I do. But not right away." She bit her lip, then decided to tell him the whole truth. "I help my family out. It's the only way my mom can manage. Brian doesn't know. Well, it's none of his business at the moment, of course, but my finances would be if we got married."

Dean was nodding across from her, his gray eyes serious behind the thick lenses. "And he wouldn't like you helping your mom?"

"I haven't asked him, but I don't think so." Brian was in such a hurry to build a nest egg and get established— as though he could fast-track his way to wealth and social position. Of course, he'd been delighted to help her with her own nest egg, and took almost as much pride as she did in watching it grow.

In fact, she realized she was overdue for a bank statement. She'd have to call and check on it. She sighed.

"He's probably not going to be very supportive of the idea of helping my family." She smiled. "I can't believe I'm telling you this stuff, things I haven't shared with Brian. You're a good listener."

"Your family is your family," Dean said. "Any man who loves you ought to see that you're a better person for helping them out."

"Oh, I—"

"No. I mean it. I'd think a lot less of someone who didn't help out their loved ones." He chuckled suddenly and she was startled at the change.

He really did have beautiful eyes, especially when they were smiling.

"What's so funny?" she asked, feeling herself smile back at him.

"Just that here I am spouting family values and I had a huge fight with my father. That's why I'm out here."

"Do you want to talk about it?" she asked, realizing the least she could do was lend him a sympathetic ear when he'd just done the same for her.

Dean shook his head as though he had something stuck in his ear. "No. I can't believe I said that. It's a stupid thing. My father and I..." He leaned back and appeared to be thinking deeply. "We want different things, I guess, but we are so much alike we butt heads. I needed to get out and do something all on my own."

She nodded enthusiastically. "I completely understand. I love my family, but I'd go crazy if I had to move back there."

"You'd rather put up with a rude neighbor?" he teased.

"You're not so bad once you stop slamming doors in my face."

"Ouch. Can't believe I ever did that. Thanks for giving me another chance."

The wine bottle was empty and the night advanced when Kate realized they had talked for hours over the dinner table. And oddly, they had talked mostly about her life, not his. What a difference from a date with Brian. Not that this was a date, of course, but still it was nice to know there were men who occasionally thought of something besides themselves.

The ringing phone jarred the cozy atmosphere, and Kate jumped up.

"Oh, hi, Brian," Kate said, wondering if he had telepathically read her mind. "How was the game tonight?" She didn't get a chance to say anything more than "Uh-huh" and "Good for you" for several minutes. She could hear the background noises of a busy bar.

Brian's voice was slightly thick, presumably from post game celebrating. He said, "Look, I've been thinking...well, I want to talk to you. I thought I'd come over."

Kate glanced at the clock on the stove. "But, Brian, it's after eleven. I've got the early shift tomorrow."

"Need to talk to you," he said. At least she thought that's what he said. The words were difficult to make out.

So much for taking a break from each other, she thought in irritation. So much for giving her some space and time to think things through.

There was no point explaining that to him in his current state. She tapped the counter, then said, "Why don't you call me tomorrow? We can talk then."

When she finished the call, Dean was stacking dishes in the kitchen.

Kate felt another jolt of shock. Brian would have walked away from the table and put the TV on to the stock market update until she'd finished clearing up.

Dean glanced up as she came into the kitchen rolling up her sleeves. "Everything okay?" he asked casually.

Kate shrugged as she slipped her rubber gloves on. "Sure. I think so."

They stood companionably side by side while Kate washed the dishes and Dean dried them. Mostly they were silent. The steamy water was causing her hair to frizz around her face. Irritably, she pushed at it with a rubber wrist.

Dean watched this gesture attentively, as though trying to see to her roots. Did he think she dyed it? She turned to face him. "It's natural, you know."

"What?" He appeared shocked.

"The color—nobody ever *asks* for red hair."

"It's not *red*, Ms. Beauty Consultant. Even I know that. It's auburn, or maybe chestnut. It reminds me of an antique mahogany table of my mom's that has this incredible rich color when candlelight hits it." He reached out and twirled a corkscrew around his finger, holding it under the light so it glowed. "That's what your hair looks like."

"Oh." Talkative Kate found herself at a loss for words. The dishes done, she stripped off the rubber gloves and began putting the dried dishes away.

Dean leaned against the counter fooling with the dish towel.

"Would you like coffee?" she asked politely.

He smiled at her. "I happen to know you've got the early shift. I'll take a rain check."

Still he didn't leave. Finally he said, "I know it's none of my business, but don't get pushed into anything by Brian, okay?"

Quick anger flared within Kate. "What do you take me for?" she snapped, turning toward him, hands firmly planted on her hips. "A complete idiot?"

He was smiling down at her, a warm light in his gray eyes. "No," he said softly. "I take you for a beautiful woman with a kind heart." He kissed her speechless lips quickly and left.

Kate stared at the closed door for long moments, her fingers touching her tingling lips.

7

THE CHAMPAGNE CORK popped and a ragged cheer went up.

"We did it, gentlemen, with hours to spare." Harvey Shield was smiling, the champagne bottle wobbling in his bony hand as he splashed foaming liquid into eight hastily wiped coffee mugs.

Darren took his mug with a nod of thanks. The effervescent fizz was loud in his ears as he idly watched the little bubbles race to the surface of the liquid popping and spurting to freedom.

He glanced around at the other programmers, God, what a pathetic bunch they were, all suffering from too much work and fast food and not enough sleep or fresh air. But they had beaten their deadline.

Darren, the newest member of the team, took as much pride in that fact as any of them. More in fact. He had already proved a few things to himself about making it on his own.

Now he had two weeks to devote entirely to his own project. Every one on the team had been offered an overtime bonus or time off. Darren hadn't hesitated. He was badly behind on his self-imposed work schedule for his educational software and he intended to spend the next two weeks catching up.

"If any of you would care to accompany me to Vincenzo's, the pizza's on me," Harvey announced, well into his third mug of champagne. There was stunned silence for a moment. Harvey's tightfistedness was a standing joke among the team.

"Great, I'll come!"

"Count me in!" called Gord and Steve in unison.

"It's all right for you single fellows, but I'm afraid the little woman will be expecting me," said Joseph Goode with his usual superior smirk. "In fact, I'd better be on my way. I thought I'd stop and pick up a little bottle of something on my way home."

"Scope or Listerine?" muttered Steve.

"Dean, you coming?" asked Gord.

"No, thanks. I'm heading straight home to bed."

"Got some hot babe warming it up for you?" Steve asked with a wink.

"Don't I wish," Darren replied. Unbidden, his imagination conjured a vision of Kate in his bed, her full curves accentuated by the silk camisole. He wished he'd never bought the damned thing. It was playing way too many tricks on his mind.

It was two weeks since he'd had dinner at her place. Two weeks of long working days and zombie sleep. Too many nights of Kate intruding on his thoughts and dreams. She was like the proverbial oasis in the middle of the desert.

And Darren was one thirsty guy.

It was odd, because he'd hardly seen her since that night, but he would hear snatches of sound from downstairs and wonder what she was doing; then lay restless in his bed thinking X-rated thoughts.

The awful truth was he wanted her. At first he'd assumed it was the combination of being away from his usual lifestyle and sharing the premises with a sexy redhead. Now that he'd come to know her better, he knew it was Kate he wanted—not a willing body at the same address, but Kate Monahan with her big green eyes, crazy hair, colorful wardrobe and sweet disposition.

Unfortunately, he had made himself as undesirable as possible, to keep women away.

What an arrogant ass.

How was he now supposed to get Kate interested in him without giving himself away? Could such a beautiful, sexy woman ever be interested in a geek?

Driving home along the darkening rain-slick streets, he pondered the problem. It was only in appearance that he'd changed. If Kate was so shallow she couldn't look deeper than appearances and appreciate the man he was inside, did he really want her, anyway?

His body answered that question for him. *Yes. God, yes.*

His beige clunkmobile screeched when he braked at a red light, then sat there rattling like an old steam engine. Not for the first time, Darren wished he was back in his BMW with a top-of-the-line CD player.

He wondered when it had rained, then thought it might have been raining on and off for a couple of days. Since he worked all the time, he tended to lose track of the weather. Though he had managed to notice that it rained a lot more out here in the Pacific Northwest than it did at home, even in the summer.

He supposed the rain was needed to water the honking great cedars and firs that grew out here. *Rain forest* was an apt description, he thought as the wipers made another desultory swipe across his windshield.

Fingers tapping on the plastic steering wheel, he surveyed the cars idling on either side of him. There was a silver Taurus station wagon on the left. Inside its respectable interior, a pair of grunge teens snuggled. The guy must have borrowed his parents' car, Darren thought with a smile, watching the black-clad, rainbow-haired teens necking with such enthusiasm they'd steamed up the windows.

Giving the kids some privacy, he shifted his attention to his right and saw a middle-aged couple chatting in a Lexus. They were less passionate than the teens, but still gave off the definite aura of two people who belonged together. They were dressed for an evening out, theater, maybe, or dinner.

With a sour pang, Darren realized it was Friday night. Date night, it seemed, for everyone but him. He glanced at the empty beige vinyl seat beside him, and knew who he wished was sitting in it, her hair a wild cloud, her green eyes sparkling. If Kate were here he'd try to act sophisticated like the Lexus couple, all the time wishing he was wrapped around her like the teen in the Taurus.

The light changed and he sputtered along behind the other cars. Up ahead he glimpsed a row of neon signs advertising every fast food known to man. On impulse, he decided to stop at a Chinese place and order takeout for two. After all, he was hungry, alone, and it was Friday night. He'd invite Kate up for dinner and start getting to know her better.

He had to admit his plan to hide in Seattle from all

womankind was working far too well. Instead of being mobbed by women who wanted to marry him, he was a lonely guy without a date on a Friday night.

He hadn't been able to stop thinking about Kate since she'd cooked him dinner. He must have wanted a woman more in his life, but he simply couldn't remember when. Probably he was close to fixated on this one because of the odd circumstances of him being forced into voluntary exile and her living at the same address.

Whatever the reason, he wanted her, and badly.

An impromptu shared take-out meal was a start. Maybe once she got to know him....

He stopped at a take-out place he'd discovered was pretty good and went for a standard combo for two.

The brown paper bag containing the stacked cardboard containers oozed steamy fragrance—and more—Darren discovered when he arrived home. As he removed the bag from the car, something wet and sticky dribbled down his pant leg.

"Aw, yuck," he cried, opening the bag and grabbing one of the paper napkins. He leaned over, dabbing at the wet mess on his pants, which made his glasses slide down his nose.

As he reached to push the damn things back up, the bottom of the soggy bag gave way. He lunged to catch the tumbling cardboard cartons and his feet hit something wet and slipped out from under him. With a thump he fell into a big, splashy, Seattle puddle.

He was so stunned he sat there for a moment in a scramble of egg foo young and chicken chow mein.

He hadn't even had time to straighten the glasses

hanging sideways down his face when the door of Kate's apartment opened and she emerged.

With a man.

Her eyes widened when she spotted Darren. Then she was running forward. "Are you all right?"

The fellow behind her was not so polite. He didn't even try to stow his grin.

Darren nodded in answer to Kate's question and glared up at the other guy. Kate's date was about Darren's own age, maybe a little younger. He looked like an ad for the rising young executive. In fact, Darren, who knew advertising, could almost believe this guy had copied everything from his medium-brown stylish hair to his shiny shoes from a layout Darren himself might have approved. He wore an expensive summer-weight jacket over a designer T-shirt. His khakis were pressed. He looked like a man who was projecting an image that wasn't natural to him—and Darren was in a position to know.

"Brian, this is Dean," Kate said.

"Hi," said Brian, having looked at Darren and his loser car and obviously decided he didn't rate a handshake. Fine by him.

"Hi."

Brian.

Of course. It was date night after all; he should have figured Kate would be going out. She'd said she was taking a break from the guy, but maybe the break was over. His night took another turn downhill.

He struggled to his feet, raining food and vegetation onto the driveway. A plump shrimp plopped onto his shoe.

Kate ran forward and squatted amongst the ruin of his evening, picking up the unopened cartons.

He grabbed the stuff from her with a curt thanks.

She was wearing a sexy little sundress and her hair was bundled on top of her head, but little corkscrews slipped out here and there, making him long to pull the whole mass of curls free.

What was she doing with a guy like Brian who showed off an expensive watch when he checked the time twice in as many minutes. If he had the money for a fancy time piece, couldn't Brian find a way to ease the life of the woman he supposedly loved? Kate worked too hard, and if he were the man in her life, Darren would try to make her life easier.

Kate smiled at him, a compassionate, friendly smile. "Have a nice evening," she said and turned away.

"Sure. You, too."

Brian slipped a possessive arm over her shoulder and walked her to the silver BMW at the curb. Sure, it was the least expensive model, but still, Brian's expensive tastes annoyed Darren when any fool could see Kate was pinching pennies to help her family and get the life she wanted.

Darren's hands squeezed into fists and another carton tumbled to the ground. His god-awful trousers clung in damp patches to his skin as he trudged slowly up to his apartment, alone and no longer hungry.

Not for Chinese food, anyway.

WOULD YOU LIKE another drink before dinner?" Brian asked Kate as he waggled his empty martini glass at the waitress behind the bar.

"No, thanks," she said, and took another sip of a margarita she wasn't enjoying. Lunch had been a granola bar snatched between a perm and streaks and as nice as the piano bar was, she wanted to get their table and eat dinner. A headache was starting to form behind her eyeballs. She wanted to enjoy the nice restaurant, but she was a little uneasy. Brian was avoiding eye contact and was fidgety. Did he want to break up permanently? If so, she wished he'd get it over with.

When she considered the idea, her heart didn't hurt at all. She didn't even hear the ding of a dent. When had her feelings changed?

Suddenly, she wanted to get this evening over with. When the waitress returned with his drink, Kate said, "Do you think we could move to our table, Brian? I'm starving."

"Oh, right," he said, taking a quick gulp and putting down the drink. "Whatever the lady wants."

It was better when they were sitting at a quiet table and her food was in front of her. Brian had ordered wine and was already well into it, but she was more interested in her salmon done with local berries and wild rice cakes. With her stomach no longer gnawing at her for attention, she could relax a bit.

Brian picked at his food, and she doubted he even knew what he was eating. Well, if she was going to get dumped, she'd like to get on with it, she decided.

"Brian, is there something on your mind?"

He opened his mouth. Closed it. Picked up his wineglass and drank. Then, with an air of casualness that she didn't buy at all, he said, "I'll tell you about it after dinner."

But she didn't want to wait in suspense. She put down her knife and fork and gave him an encouraging smile. It was better to get this over with, she decided. Maybe then they could continue as friends. "I'd rather hear whatever it is, now. Really. You'll feel better when it's out in the open."

"You sound as if you know what I have to tell you."

"I've got some ideas," she said. They'd been taking a break from each other, and now, out of the blue, he wanted a date? Sure, she had some ideas.

He reached over and took her hand. His felt surprisingly hot and a little clammy. He pulled back, shifted in his seat and said, "There's a bit of a problem with your account at the bank. It's no big deal, but I wanted to tell you about it myself."

"What kind of problem?" She kept her voice calm, but Brian looked very red in the face for something that was no big deal. Her head throbbed louder like a warning drum.

"It's down a little bit, that's all."

"Down a little bit?" The words came out high and sharp. "Brian, it's invested in certificates of deposit. That's the safest investment there is. How could it be down?"

"CDs are for chumps. I played the market for you a little bit. I didn't tell you because I didn't want you to worry. We'll be fine. We'll come back. It's just down a little right now. Temporarily." His tone was jaunty, but his expression was guilty.

There was no point reminding him that money was for her future. She'd been saving up for college. He knew that. And she'd always been clear that she wasn't interested in gambling or quick returns. She worked darned hard for her money and she'd take a low interest rate any day before she'd risk losing her principal.

Facts, she told herself. She needed facts before she went off the deep end.

"How much is my account down?"

"About nine Gs."

Her heart thumped uncomfortably against her ribs. "Nine thousand dollars?" That was more than a third of her money and it had taken her a long time to save it.

"Look, I'll put it back, I promise."

"Put it back?" She stared at him as the light began to dawn. She'd signed some kind of papers that he'd said would make it easier for him to reinvest her money without her having to come into the bank every time a CD came due. She hadn't paid a lot of attention to the wording because she'd trusted Brian. Now she realized how badly she'd misjudged him.

"You didn't gamble with the money in my account, did you? You took it out. You must have."

"Sure. But I did it for you, babe. For us. For our future," he said, sounding desperately eager to be believed, which made her certain he was lying.

"Where did you put my money?"

"The stock market. I had some good tips and I was already overextended in my own accounts. I borrowed some cash from you, that's all."

"No," she said, rising and placing her napkin carefully on the table beside her half-finished dinner. "You didn't. You took money that didn't belong to you. You stole my money, Brian. And you need to decide what you're going to do about it."

She turned and started walking.

"Wait! Don't go."

She ignored him, walking around a table where a couple was holding hands and gazing at each other, obviously having a more successful evening than she. Kate walked carefully toward the door feeling as though the floor had tilted beneath her feet. Funny, she was a woman of hot temper usually, but right now she felt cold. Maybe nine thousand dollars wasn't a lot of money to some people, but it was a hell of a lot to her.

Soon she'd be angry, she knew she would, but right now she was too stunned to feel much of anything, except the need to get home.

"Kate. Where are you going? Kate!"

Fortunately, there was a cab just arriving at the curb. She hurried over to it, and as a couple of laughing young women left, she got in and slammed the door. She heard Brian shout something, but again she ignored him.

By the time the cab pulled up in front of her apartment she was feeling again. And as angry as she was with Brian, she heaped a load of hot fury onto her own head. How could she have been such a fool?

She hadn't even got the door of her suite open when she heard the squeal of tires in her drive and knew without bothering to turn that Brian was there. On top of stealing, he was drinking and driving. What a prince.

"Kate, you have to listen."

She turned and regarded him levelly. "I don't have to do anything."

"I know you're mad. Go ahead. Yell at me. But this is

only a temporary setback. I'll get that money back. I promise I will."

She was amazed at how cool she was. He'd be only too pleased if she started yelling, she thought. He knew she had a quick temper. But shouting wasn't going to get her anywhere, and she found she didn't want a fight with Brian. She didn't want anything with him. "I'll be changing banks," she informed him.

"Please, please listen to me." He sounded desperate. "You can't tell anyone at the bank. I'll lose my job if you do. Please." He followed her inside, leaving the door open, and that was the final straw.

Now she yelled at him, good and loud.

"I did not invite you in. Get out!"

Ignoring her arm pointing toward the door, he came forward. His face was as pale as it had been red earlier, and his hands were shaking as he reached for her. "Please. Give me some time."

"I said, get out."

"Not until you promise—"

"I believe you were asked to leave," said a welcome voice. Her shouting must have brought him downstairs at a run, for he was panting slightly, taking in the scene at a glance.

Brian turned slowly. "Why don't you mind your own business?" he said, swaying slightly. The three martinis and all that wine must be catching up with him.

Dean held the door open with all the politeness of a maître d' at a five-star restaurant. "Do us all a favor. Go home and sleep it off."

Brian grabbed the door and pushed hard, obviously trying to shut Dean out. "I am having a conversation with the woman I'm going to marry," he said through gritted teeth as he pushed against the door that wasn't budging.

Dean's gaze lifted swiftly to hers, and she shook her head, a little pity seeping in under her anger. "No, you're not going to marry me, Brian. It's over."

The minute she voiced the words, Dean said, "Do you want me to turf him for you?"

She was about to say no when Brian let go of the door and jumped back so Dean was propelled inside. "I'll do the turfing, got it? Everything was fine until you moved in, and it was 'Dean this,' and 'Dean that.' I'm sick of hearing about you. You pencil-necked geek." And then Brian, who ought to be groveling at her feet, suddenly rushed forward and aimed a fist at her neighbor.

Dean dodged the drunken blow and moved away from the door, then glanced at her. "Go on up to my place, Kate. The door's open."

Brian took advantage of his momentary lapse in attention to run at him.

Kate clapped her hand over her mouth to stop herself screeching. She had seen her brothers in enough fights in her time to know that the best thing she could do was to keep quiet and stay out of the way. But she had no intention of running up to Dean's apartment and leaving him alone with Brian.

Her ex was an athletic guy who played a lot of sports. She couldn't bear it if Dean, whose only contact sport seemed to be tapping his fingers against his keyboard, got hurt. She crept toward the phone.

She was watching a classic scene of the intellectual nice guy standing up to the schoolyard bully.

Dean had jumped clear of Brian once again, but he'd obviously given up trying to get him out of her apartment without a fight. The two men started circling each other, like dogs fighting over a bone.

And she was the bone.

Her eyes stung. She wasn't about to watch a gentle man she liked get beaten to a pulp for trying to stand up for her.

Brian lunged again, and suddenly fists were flying, furniture crashing. She heard the sickening grunts as fists swung into soft flesh. She picked up the telephone receiver, hoping the police would get there fast.

Her hand was shaking. She punched 91—and then the receiver went flying as a body banged into her. She bit back a yelp and made a run for the kitchen. Dean needed help. If she couldn't get the cops, then she could grab her rolling pin and pitch in herself.

"Go upstairs, Kate!" Dean's voice was stronger, more commanding than she'd ever heard it.

She gaped at him, and suddenly noticed that it wasn't her neighbor who was getting the worst of the fight, but Brian. He was sweating and breathing in short, ragged gasps while Dean's breathing seemed closer to normal than when he'd first burst in on the scene.

She forgot about the rolling pin and tried to take in the amazing spectacle.

Dean didn't attack, she noticed, but waited for Brian to come at him, and then defended himself with an aggressiveness that left his assailant winded and bruised. One of Brian's eyes was rapidly closing and his nose was bleeding in a steady dribble. He seemed stunned, unable to believe the fight would not go his way.

A flicker of amusement crossed Dean's strong, reliable face, "Had enough?"

"Go to hell." Brian's eyes narrowed. He lowered his head and charged. With swinging fists, Dean sent the grunting, panting Brian stumbling toward the door and with a mighty push sent him sprawling. She thought he'd aimed Brian toward the still-open door, but the other man's foot connected with an overturned chair and he hit the window. She heard the crack of glass. As Brian tried to right himself, his elbow connected with the crack and the window ended up with a gaping hole in it.

Dean grabbed his opponent by the front of his shirt, pulled him back from the window and this time when he shoved, Brian landed outside.

Right on his ass.

Then Dean slammed the door behind him and locked it. Still he stayed there alert until they both heard the roar of the car's engine and the sound of Brian driving away.

Now that it was over, the adrenaline and anger that had fueled her seemed to drain. Dean's feet and legs moved into her line of vision, white blurs on the green background. She watched them move purposely toward her and then hesitate a few feet away. He spoke to her quietly.

"Come upstairs. I'll make you some tea."

It was an effort to look up.

He stood with his hand held out, a comforting smile on his face.

She hesitated for a moment and then clasped his hand.

He held on to her all the way up the stairs and into his apartment, not letting go until she was seated on the couch. Then he went into the kitchenette and made tea. The opening of cupboards, the whistling of the kettle— the sounds of a person moving around a kitchen—were normal, everyday sounds that made her so glad he was here.

Soon she held a steaming mug in her hands. Not anemic herbal tea, thank God, but thick dark tea like her ma would make. When she sipped the scalding liquid, she felt the burn all the way down into her stomach. "What is in here?" she spluttered.

"Brandy. You looked like you needed it."

She sipped the doctored tea, letting the brandy burn its way down. Finally she looked up to find him regarding her with compassion. He'd taken off the awful glasses, leaving two red dents on either side of his nose. There weren't any other marks on his face, no bruises or cuts. Apart from some redness on his knuckles, he looked normal.

"Where did you learn to fight?" she had to ask.

There was a pause. She thought he wasn't going to answer her.

His voice was so low she could hardly hear the words. "Boxing team. University," he mumbled to the floor, as though he were ashamed.

If she hadn't seen him in action she never would have believed it. "I thought boxers needed good eyesight?"

He squirmed in his chair. "I don't need glasses all the time." His hair flopped forward, hiding his expression.

"Lucky for me you took boxing," she said. "You're a good neighbor." She thought for a moment of Annie, her much mourned former upstairs tenant. Maybe Dean wasn't as much fun on wash day, but she couldn't imagine Annie decking Brian quite so effectively.

His gaze caught hers. "I hope we're more than neighbors."

"Of course. We're friends." Impulsively, she crossed to him and kissed his cheek. There was a pleasant scrape of whiskers against her cheek and he smelled good. Like soap and clean male, with an overtone of the healthy sweat of a workout. Boxing, huh? "Thanks."

She placed the empty cup down on the cheap wooden coffee table that came with the place. "I'd better get back downstairs."

He rose as well, shaking his head firmly. "You can't sleep down there with a broken window. Tonight you'll sleep up here. I'll take the couch."

"But..." The protest stopped before it started. She read the concern on his face and knew that it wasn't cold he was worried about. He thought Brian might return.

Would he? Who knew. The man had gone from apologetic to belligerent awfully quickly. Maybe he'd come back to try again to convince her not to pull her money or go to the bank administration and tell her story.

No. She didn't want to face Brian again tonight, and she certainly didn't want Dean to have to act as her bouncer a second time.

"I'm going down now to put some cardboard in the window. Do you want to get your things?"

She nodded.

She was going to cry. She knew it as surely as she knew rain would follow a violent storm.

Holding the tears at bay, she followed Dean down the stairs and into her apartment. She grabbed her night things, then stopped to swallow a couple of pain killers for the headache still pounding behind her eyeballs.

She didn't cry when she went around her apartment righting furniture, clearing up the broken glass and crushed flowers, and inspecting the damage to her plants. Dean was there, cutting up a cardboard box and patching the window, and she had her pride.

She didn't cry when she washed and changed in his bathroom and emerged to find him bundling a pile of sheets out of his bedroom. He had changed the bedsheets for her, she realized, and that small courtesy was almost her undoing. She bit her lip hard.

At last she lay in bed in Dean's spartan room, in his double bed with a plaid bedcover that looked as though it had come from a discount store. A box with some extra computer equipment sat on his dresser. On his bedside table was a lamp, a box of tissues, a cheap clock radio and a pair of socks. That was it. There was nothing personal in the room. No pictures of family, no posters on the walls. It was as impersonal as a hotel room.

How bizarre.

Even more bizarre, the room felt comforting, she realized. There was something about Dean that made her relax. Not relaxed enough to forget she'd had a good chunk of her savings stolen, though, but a hell of a lot more relaxed than she'd be downstairs with nothing but a broken window and misery for company.

She waited until it was dark and quiet and she could hold her tears back no longer, then they came. She put the pillow over her head to muffle the little snuffling sobs that shook her—clenching her fingers against the pillow in impotent rage and grief.

She hadn't only lost her money, but her dreams, and her faith in a man she'd trusted.

She didn't hear the door open, she only knew Dean was in the room when she felt the tentative comforting touch on her shoulder. He pulled the pillow gently away and stroked her hair in long, soothing motions.

She sat up, pushing the tangle of hair out of her eyes. "I'm s-so s-sorry," she sobbed as he drew her gently into his arms. "I can't h-help it."

"It's okay," he said. "Shove over." So she did, and he sat on top of the bed and put an arm around her shoulders.

She resisted for a moment, but the broad shoulder was there beside her cheek, warm and comforting. She lay her head against it and sobbed her heart out while he held her and stroked her hair and murmured soothingly.

The storm of weeping passed and she lay quiet in his arms, noticing that she had thrown her arms around him and was clinging to him as though she were drowning in stormy seas and he were a lifeboat.

She relaxed her hold and felt the swelling and receding of his chest as he breathed. She again smelled the soap and clean male skin. Against her cheek his bathrobe was warm and soft. Where it gaped in a vee in the middle, she glimpsed a muscled chest sprinkled with dark hair. Out of nowhere came an insane urge to slip her hand inside the robe and touch him.

What was wrong with her?

One man had betrayed her and she was throwing

herself at her neighbor just because he was being nice to her? She really needed to get a grip.

She pulled away, sniffing. "Thanks, Dean." She felt suddenly shy as she dropped her gaze from the lean, muscular chest, only to see his lean, muscular legs emerging from the bottom of his robe. She shoved her hands over her eyes and rubbed away the wetness. "I'm better now."

He reached behind him and handed her the box of tissues she'd noted earlier.

While she blew her nose and wiped her eyes, he said, "Do you want to talk about it?"

Did she? There was something so easy about Dean. He was trustworthy and decent, and she knew she'd feel better if she unloaded some of her anger, so she told him.

"I gave Brian power of attorney over my investment account at his bank." She stopped and blew her nose again. "It was a convenience thing so I wouldn't have to go in every time I had a CD come due. It's all I bought in that account. I wanted safe investments."

She bit her lip and wondered if she could say the next part without bawling again.

The house was so silent she could hear the rustle of bedclothes as Dean shifted slightly, hear his breathing and the sounds of the duplex settling for the night.

"I'm listening."

"Brian took some of the money out."

"He did what?" Dean sounded as outraged as she felt. Whatever he'd suspected, it clearly hadn't been that.

"He said he invested it for me for a higher return, but

that's not true. He took the money right out of the account for his own use." She swallowed hard to prevent another outbreak of tears.

"What was he doing with it?"

"Playing the stock market. He was always trying to get rich quick."

"I bet he sucks at stock picking. Those kinds of guys usually do."

She laughed weakly. "I'm guessing you're right. I feel so *stupid*."

Dean hugged her hard. "Brian's the one who stole. Don't get down on yourself. This is his fault. Let's work on getting that money back."

"He's promised he'll return what he took—stole—but he's already lied and cheated. I find it hard to believe him, you know?"

Dean seemed to hesitate, then asked, "Was it a lot of money?"

"A third of my life savings. I know it could be worse, but I have plans, dreams. He knew that."

He played with her hair absently and she found the gesture amazingly soothing. "He sounds to me like a sneaky bastard. He made sure he had a legal right to invest your money in stocks. Of course, it was totally unethical since he went against your specific wishes. I think it's worth filing an official complaint against him, though."

"I know I was gullible. But he stole my dreams."

"If you let me, I'm going to help you get them back."

She leaned into him, letting herself take the comfort that she needed.

"It helps knowing I can talk to you."

"Well, that's something." He sounded a little sad, but she figured it was on her account.

"'Night, Kate."

"'Night." She looked at him. There was so little light in the room she could only barely see him, but even so she found she couldn't look away.

Dean tilted her chin up and she shivered slightly. Then he leaned forward and kissed her. Not enough for passion, but a little more than friendship.

She didn't move, couldn't, suddenly wondering where this was going. Where she wanted it to go.

Then he was gone. Before she quite realized he'd stopped kissing her, he was out the door.

8

KATE EASED OPEN the lid of the florist box as though a nest of snakes lay coiled inside. There were at least three dozen long-stemmed red roses crammed in the box. Her stomach constricted when she read the card.

Please forgive me. I love you. Brian.

She wished she'd been home to refuse the delivery, but she'd been at work blaming her puffy red eyes and pale cheeks on a head cold. Averting her gaze from the blood-red flowers, she marched to the garbage can, but when she opened the lid she couldn't bring herself to destroy the fresh blooms. It wasn't their fault Brian was pond scum.

Forgiveness? Was that what he really wanted? Or was he hoping a few flowers and even more flowery words would stop her reporting him to his bank's management.

Irresolute, she stood for a moment with the green plastic lid in one hand and the box of roses in the other. Finally she threw the note in the trash and drove the roses to a local seniors' home.

"A donation," she told a puzzled receptionist.

The woman glanced at her face and flashed a sympathetic smile. "From a funeral, dear?"

She smiled back, feeling her lips tremble. "Yes," she whispered. It was a funeral, all right. For all her foolish dreams. Why *had* she trusted Brian in the first place? She thought about that as she made her way home slowly. Maybe she'd bought into his plans to go places—he'd seemed to her the epitome of a confident man with a successful future, and she'd been flattered that he'd seen her as part of his future, and happy to be part of his success. Did she have so little confidence in herself?

But Brian had changed. It had been gradual, but when she'd told him they needed to take a break from each other, she'd heeded some voice inside her that recognized all was not right with him. When first they'd started seeing each other, he'd been a social drinker, but the last six months or so he'd been drinking more. She'd imagined it was the stress of his work, and maybe it was, but maybe it was also part of whatever had caused him to change from a fun-loving and kind, if self-involved guy, to a man who would borrow her savings without permission.

Her ex-boyfriend would have done better to have a new window delivered than a bunch of flowers, Kate thought, when she arrived back home. She'd been lucky to find a company that would replace the glass the same day she called, but the gleaming new pane had made another dent in her savings.

Now, on the outside, everything looked the same as it had yesterday. Including Kate. But inside she wondered how she could ever have been so blind.

There were stories in the newspapers and on TV all the time about people being conned out of their savings, and she'd always thanked her lucky stars she wasn't the kind to be taken in so easily. Now she wondered about her own judgment.

The phone was ringing when she entered her apartment. She knew who was calling and she hesitated, letting it ring, then decided to get the call over with. Her heart sank as she picked up the receiver. "Hello?"

"Oh, baby, I'm so sorry. Please forgive me." Brian's voice sounded hoarse.

"Have you stolen from all your clients? Or is it just me?" Her voice was cold and surprisingly steady since she simmered inside with hurt and anger. She hadn't decided yet what she was going to do next, but if there were other people involved, she'd have no choice but to report him.

"I didn't touch anyone else's account. I swear I didn't. And I didn't steal your money. I admit, I got in over my head. Damn market. But I bought those stocks in your name, for you. They just haven't come back up yet is all."

How typical, she thought, to blame the market for his troubles.

"So you played the market with my money, even though you knew I only wanted the safest investments."

He sighed heavily. "I screwed up. I didn't have the money to buy the stocks myself and I hated the thought of your money sitting there making a couple of measly percentage points when we could do a lot better."

"You didn't do better, though, did you. You lost the money."

"I thought I could put it back before you found out. I will get it back to you, I swear it."

She found vengeance hard to mete out to a man she'd once considered marrying. Somehow, she kept remembering the old days, when he'd been so different. "I'll give you one week."

"Please don't hang up." He was crying. She could hear the snuffling sound coming from the receiver. "I never meant to hurt you. Please, Kate, just give me another chance."

"Brian, go to AA. If you're still sober in six months, call me. In the meantime, all I want is my money back." No, she thought, that wasn't all she wanted. Some part of her knew he wasn't a bad man, but a weak and foolish one with a problem. "I'm serious. I think you need some help. If you keep going down this path you'll lose your career and all your plans for the future. Now, please don't call me again."

"Wait, Kate, I'm sorry. Please can't we—"

"If you're really sorry, you'll take my advice. You have a drinking problem. Do something about it."

She clicked the phone down. And grabbed the receiver again immediately, punching buttons rapidly. "Ruby! Can you come over tonight?"

It was her best friend's day off, so Kate hadn't been able to get her levelheaded take on the whole situation. Which, right now, was what she needed.

"Sorry, honey. I got me a hot date."

"Oh..." She tried not to sound as though she would collapse on the floor in hysterics if her friend didn't come over, even though that's how she felt. "Good for you. Have fun."

"Hey, everything okay?"

Kate put on a false cheeriness. "Yeah, sure. See you tomorrow. You can tell me all about your date then."

Hanging up, she listened to the silence. She glanced around the small apartment and knew she didn't want to be alone. She didn't want to go out and face noisy crowds, either. She just wanted a friend. Ruby was busy, and there wasn't anyone else she could talk to about this...

Dean was her friend.

The thought struck home, and she realized with a shock that it was true. After last night, they'd moved beyond neighbors. The nerdy computer guy upstairs had been there when she needed him and she knew instinctively she could trust him.

From what she'd seen, living in the same building, he didn't have much of a social life. Maybe he'd be interested in a movie? She ran to the new window and glanced out, but his car wasn't in the driveway.

She dropped the curtain back in place, fighting yet another urge to cry. It looked like she was spending the evening alone.

She padded into the kitchen and yanked open the fridge door. Yogurt, vegetables, fruit. Blah. There was a time for health food, and there was a time for junk food and wine. Tonight was made for junk food.

Trouble was, she didn't have any.

A quick survey of her cupboards revealed half a bottle of cooking sherry. She pulled the cork, sniffed and jerked her nose away. Okay, she didn't have any wine, either.

With a sigh, she slopped some yogurt into a bowl and

wandered back into the living room, where she collapsed onto the couch.

If she couldn't have junk food and wine, the next best thing would be an old black-and-white tearjerker. She turned on the TV and started flicking channels. Nature shows, sports, sitcom reruns—her spirits sank lower. She finally settled on a documentary about the disappearing rain forest. She figured it would be as depressing as any tearjerker, and at least it was educational.

The ringing doorbell made her jump, torn between dread that it was Brian and hope that Ruby had changed her mind.

A sigh of relief burst from her lips when she saw the familiar face, the glasses made huge by the distorting lens of the peephole.

She opened the door and smiled.

Dean held out a big pizza box and a bottle in a paper bag. "Could I interest you in dinner for two?" he said.

Her smile widened. "I've never been so happy to see anybody. Come on in."

The night didn't seem so lonely, or her situation so desperate, all of a sudden.

Dean was such an easy person to be around, Kate thought, as she munched the fully loaded pizza and sipped red wine. She'd expected to feel a twinge of embarrassment when she saw him again, after the way she'd cried all over him last night. But he acted so much like he always did, kind of sweet and shy, that her heart warmed to him, and the embarrassment never materialized.

"He played the market with my money."

The pizza box was empty, the wine bottle nearly so—

and Kate had a pretty good idea she'd had more than her fair share of the latter—before she brought up the subject they'd both been avoiding.

Dean didn't say a word, just nodded.

Kate looked down at the last of the red wine in the bottom of her glass, at the tiny crimson waves rolling across the surface.

"He called today and told me he'd played my money because he didn't have enough of his own that wasn't tied up. He says he'll pay it back."

"What do you think?"

"I think he's changed. I may not be the world's best judge of character, but I swear the man I met two years ago wouldn't have done something like this." She shrugged. "Or maybe I simply didn't know him. I feel so stupid. I know it's partly my fault for trusting him so blindly."

Dean was standing over her in a second. She'd never seen anyone move so fast. "Would you stop that? How the hell is it your fault? Kate, all kinds of people give their brokers power over their accounts. I do it myself. You don't expect them to play stupid games and gamble with your savings."

Dean had a broker? Somehow it was hard to imagine.

Kate laughed shakily. "Thanks. I think maybe I could have handled things differently. He didn't start out like this. When we first knew each other he was sweet. But in the last couple of months he's been different...."

"Different how?"

"It's like he was living a lie. He pretended he was one person, the banker I trusted, but all the time he was someone completely different. He was using me, using my money without telling me. It was nothing but lies. That's the worst betrayal of all."

Dean made a choking sound.

"Are you all right?"

His face was all red, and he started to cough. "Wine went down the wrong way," he gasped.

She ran into the kitchen for a glass of water, which he gulped down. "Sorry. Go on about Brian."

Too restless to resume her seat, she moved to stare at the oatmeal curtains covering the new window. She thought about Brian's grandiose plans, his loud behavior with his friends, and how often she'd seen him drink too much.

Telling him to go to AA had come out of nowhere, but Kate began to think maybe it was the drinking that had caused the change.

"You know, I don't want to talk about him anymore," she suddenly said. "He's taken up enough of my time and attention. So—" she stretched her arms above her head "—I'm free. Free of a man who didn't deserve me, free of the burden of too much money," she smiled wryly. "Free to start over."

"Free to find another man," he reminded her softly.

She wrinkled her nose. "I think I'm done with men for a while."

"Don't judge us all by one creep who didn't deserve a minute of your time. You should start over."

Kate looked back at him. He sat slumped, with his back against the sofa, knees drawn up, contemplating his sneakers.

"You're a fine one to talk. The upstairs suite hasn't exactly been rocking with passion since you moved in."

He opened his mouth, then closed it with a snap. Looking down, he twiddled with his shoelaces again, his face slowly flushing deep red.

"Oh, I'm sorry, Dean. I... Talk about out of line..."

He rose to his feet, giving her a smile that was slightly off center. "That's okay. I...I am interested in someone. I just can't have the girl I want, that's all."

"I—"

He shut the empty pizza box. "It's late. I'd better be going."

"Thanks for coming tonight. It's good to know I've got a friend in the building."

"All you have to do is call." He smiled as he opened the door.

"I hope you get your girl, Dean. You deserve her," she said to his retreating back. He gave no sign of having heard her as he shut the door softly behind him.

Kate sat down and drained the rest of her glass. Dean Edgar suffering from unrequited love? It was hard to believe. She had pictured him as having a lifelong love affair with his computer, a kind of absentminded professor who barely noticed the opposite sex. It was sad to think of him pining away for a woman who probably couldn't see past the nerd. He was such a nice guy once you got to know him.

He'd been so good to her, she wished she could help him in some way.

Suddenly she sat up straight as an idea struck, so blindingly brilliant it made her gasp.

Of course! She knew exactly what she could do to help him get his woman.

Kate smiled, a wicked, mischievous smile. She was in

the beauty business, wasn't she? She knew all about helping people look their best.

What Dean Edgar needed was a makeover!

And what better way to get her mind off her own troubles than to help her new friend out of his.

The first thing she wanted to do was throw away those glasses. Surely they made contact lenses even for people with really poor vision. Uncovering Dean's fabulous gray eyes would be a big step in the right direction.

Then there was the hair. Kate's scissor fingers itched when she was around him. She wanted to give him a shorter cut, brushed away from his face instead of hanging all over it, obscuring his features.

She couldn't figure out why any hair-care professional, even the neighborhood barber, would give him a cut like that. Perhaps his ears stuck out. She'd have to check.

Closing her eyes, she tried to picture him without glasses and with a good haircut. He had even, regular features and a really charming smile. Yes, he'd be quite passable, even attractive.

Then there were the clothes. Mentally she began undressing him. Getting rid of the horrible shirts, the baggy shorts that he seemed to buy in too big a size, and the endless supply of baseball caps. And maybe if she got him feeling more confident about his appearance, he'd stand straighter.

She thought about how he'd felt when she cried on his shoulder. She'd had her arms wrapped around him, one of his around her while he'd stroked her hair.

She sank back against the sofa cushions and remembered the sensation of warmth and safety she felt—and the strength. She felt warm again at the thought of it.

The hands that had stroked her hair, offered her a tissue, were well shaped, manly hands. All that jogging—and boxing—had given him a nice muscular build. An image of his naked chest snuck into her mind.

Yes, she thought, enthusiasm building—he could be a really nice makeover. Some decent clothes, a good haircut and contact lenses, and his mystery woman would be falling at his feet.

Kate jumped up and dashed into the bedroom, straight to the bookcase where she kept her trade journals and albums. She piled a few on her nightstand, and when she was ready for bed, she curled up, flipping pages, looking for a new hairstyle for Dean. She fell asleep on top of a Brad Pitt look-alike who wore his hair cropped close above his ears and brushed back.

She smiled in her dreams.

"WHAT DO YOU MEAN YOU won't do it?" Kate wailed.

Darren watched the excited flush fade from her pink cheeks.

On his living room table an oversize professional album of men's hairstyles lay open to a picture of a *GQ*-model kind of guy in crisp short hair. "This would look great on you," Kate insisted.

Darren knew exactly how it would look. He'd worn his hair that way a year ago, before he grew it long enough to annoy his father, but not long enough to annoy himself.

Kate had an eye for her business, that was for sure. And too sharp an eye for Darren's taste.

"Thanks, but I don't think so," he said, closing the album on a picture that reminded him uncomfortably that he was the second man Kate had trusted who was living a lie.

Darren was glad he still had more than a week before he was due back at SYX Systems. He was at the duplex most of the time, which allowed him to keep an eye on Kate. In his Neanderthal heart he hoped Brian would come back, so he could have the pleasure of pounding him into the ground. In the meantime he pounded computer keys and watched Kate try to regain her confidence.

Since the night of the pizza, Darren had discovered he had a firm friend. And when Kate was your friend, it wasn't a passive "Hi, how are you doing, let's get together sometime" kind of friend; it was an active "What can I do to fix your life" kind of friend.

Now here she was, leaning forward, green eyes aglow, outlining a program to improve his image so he could get the girl of his dreams.

He almost laughed aloud.

He lived inside a disguise while the woman he wanted was eager to redo his image for a woman she didn't realize was herself. What a mess. And Kate was nothing if not tenacious.

"Look, I'm not suggesting dyeing your hair or anything."

If she only knew. He religiously touched up his roots every couple of weeks so his sharp-eyed beauty consultant neighbor would think it was God who'd given him hair the color of mud.

"I only want to update your image a bit. Maybe this

woman you like would notice you if you looked
more...um...contemporary." She sounded tentative.
Maybe she thought she might hurt his feelings. He
would play that up.

"I don't want a new image, Kate," he said as petu-
lantly as he could.

"Well, of course not. Not a new image—a more flattering look. Trust me, I know what women like. I am a
beauty consultant, remember?"

"No."

"Just let me cut your hair," she wheedled.

He hiked the glasses back up and leaned forward,
speaking earnestly the truth he felt in his heart. "Kate,
however much I care about this woman, I want her to
appreciate me for who I am. A fancy haircut, expensive
clothes, the right car, the right toys won't make me a
better person."

"Haven't you ever heard of hiding your light under a
bushel?" she shot back.

"I'm not pretending to be anything except a simple
guy who works on computers." He looked directly into
Kate's eyes. "A woman who can't look beyond the surface to the man I am inside is of no interest to me," he
said with finality. "So, no. I won't have a makeover."

He held her gaze and her green eyes widened
slightly. Her breath caught. He felt for the first time as
though she was looking at him as a man instead of a
nerd. He opened his mouth, but what he would have
said remained a mystery.

Kate drained the last of the coffee from her mug and
stood. She looked thoughtful, even a little hurt, but not

beaten. "I'll leave the book. Have another look at it, maybe you'll change your mind."

As she straightened, Darren enjoyed the way the sleeveless sweater she was wearing moved with her. It complemented her rosy cheeks and the tangled glory of her hair.

"I like your sweater," he said.

She tossed her hair back, giving him her sassiest look. "Hmm. You should like me for what's underneath."

He watched in amusement as the fiery color swept her cheeks. She must have realized how he could interpret her words.

"I meant what's inside..." Her blush intensified as she waded in deeper. "*Me* I mean, not the sweater."

"I like both," he said quietly.

Her eyes flew to his and a gasp escaped her lips.

She was an intriguing combination of sexy and shy. It amazed him that the same woman who wore those wild outfits could blush like a schoolgirl and get her tongue all tied up.

"My mother made it," she said, and rushed on. "She loves knitting and crocheting."

"I'd like to meet your family some day. They sound fascinating," he said.

"You would?" She looked frankly stunned. "Go to the zoo and look in the monkey cage, then you've seen my family. Too many primates shrieking and plucking at one another in too small a space. That's my family." She smiled. "They're a good lot, though."

"My family would never shriek. Or pluck. My mother has a rule against raised voices." He shrugged. That other life seemed so far away. It was amazing he could be so content with so relatively little. A crummy apartment, no social life, looks that had gone from metrosexual to asexual. But he had work that he loved, and an intriguing project—trying to score with the woman downstairs with none of his usual arsenal.

"I guess your life back east seems a long way away," she said.

He swung on her, sharp suspicion jabbing at him. "How did you know I'm from back east?"

She blinked at him, clearly confused by his reaction. "Aren't you? Your accent is. You sound like one of the Kennedys, so I assumed..."

"Right. Sorry." He rubbed a hand over his face. What was he thinking? If Kate had figured out he was the guy in the magazine, she'd ask him about it. She wouldn't sneak around behind his back, she wasn't that kind of woman. "I think I'm working too hard."

"Oh, right. You're working. I shouldn't have interrupted. I'll let you get back to it."

He turned to face her, realizing how churlish he'd sounded. "I wasn't trying to get rid of you. Stay."

She'd paused in the doorway, so gloriously tempting he wanted to shout *Yes. Make me over. Uncover the Match of the Year. Win the prize.*

But he knew he wouldn't.

Not because he gave a damn about the bachelor thing anymore, but because he had meant what he said.

He wanted Kate to fall for him, not because they belonged to the same clubs and had the same friends, or because her father's bank wanted his father's business, or because some magazine said he was desirable. He wanted Kate to want Dean Edgar. A man who was just as real, if not more so, than Darren Edgar Kaiser Jr.

"I've got some things to do before going to work, anyway." She glanced at the computer humming quietly on the Formica kitchen table. "How's your educational software coming?"

He made a face. "Not that well. I'm working on a game to teach kids about computers in a fun way. But everything I've come up with is too technical. No fun."

"Well, I never finished high school. So if you want to experiment on me..." She snapped her mouth closed. Darren got the feeling she wished she hadn't spoken.

"I'd appreciate your comments a lot," he said. In fact, he'd appreciate anything that allowed them to spend more time together.

She walked over to the computer and ran one pointed nail over the keyboard. "Educational software...I always wanted to be a teacher." Her voice was low and he was certain he heard pain.

He shouldn't ask. It was none of his business, but he couldn't stop himself. "Why aren't you?"

"My dad died." Her hair bounced up and down once as she shrugged her shoulders. She stared at that keyboard as if she was trying to memorize it. "No money for college."

"And no money to finish high school?" he asked gently.

She shook her head. "I was lucky to get a job in a beauty salon. Turns out I have a flair for hair." She turned to him with a big smile, and said with false heartiness, "Everybody knows beauty and brains don't go together. So I stick to beauty."

He moved toward her without thought and took her stubborn chin in his hand. He yanked his glasses off to gaze down into her troubled eyes without a chunk of glass between them. "Sometimes they do. You, for instance, are both beautiful and smart."

For a moment she gazed back, a tiny frown between her brows, as though trying to find a reason to believe him. Her skin was soft and warm, and where his baby finger rested on her neck he felt her pulse leap.

Then she pulled away with a little snort of laughter. "This from a guy who takes Bart Simpson as his fashion icon."

"You can be anything you want to be, Kate," he said, ignoring her attempt to throw his compliment back at him.

She was staring at him, the frown still lodged between her brows.

"What?"

"Sometimes you remind me of someone. I just can't get it. Is there a movie star you look like?"

Damn. His picture had been in the Seattle paper yesterday. Someone claimed to have seen him in San Francisco, and the reward for finding him had gone up. He pushed the glasses back on and hunched his shoulders. "I don't have much time for the movies."

She shook her head. "I can't place it, but you remind me of someone. Anyway, let me know if you change your mind about the haircut. I can do you in thirty minutes and it won't cost you a penny." With a wink she was gone.

Darren sat back down to the computer, but he couldn't seem to concentrate. *I can do you in thirty minutes*, she'd said. Oh no, she couldn't. The things he had in mind would take all night.

He'd never wanted anything so badly as he wanted Kate Monahan. There'd been a moment there when he could have sworn she looked at him the way a woman looks at a man. But then it had passed, and she'd gone back to acting like his helpful friend and neighbor.

What would she have done if he'd come right out and told her she was the one he was interested in? Not some mystery babe, but Kate Monahan?

With a scowl, he thumped the screen back to life. If he had to guess, he imagined she'd have got all flustered and backed away as fast as her shapely legs could carry her.

Friends was better than nothing.

All Kate's talk about her family got him to thinking about his family and their quiet, well-regulated house. A pang of guilt struck. He'd been so busy with work he hadn't written home for weeks.

He was so paranoid about being tracked that he'd stopped phoning his folks. He sent letters—minus any address or phone number—to Bart, who forwarded them to his family.

Because of his paranoia about detection, he didn't even have an e-mail address. He'd never been so out of touch with his world. The strange thing was how little he missed what was back home, and how much he'd come to care for what was here in Seattle, literally right under his nose.

His family wrote to him through Bart, who mailed their letters to an obscure post office box where Darren picked up his mail. It was as slow and antiquated as the pony express, but so far, he remained undetected.

He found paper and pen and sat down again at the kitchen table, pushing the keyboard out of the way. It was halting at first, but soon words were racing across the page as he told his family about his job and his few friends.

He tried to tell them something about Kate, but he didn't know how to describe her without giving them the wrong impression. He shouldn't care what his family made of his downstairs neighbor, but he did. He cared very much. In the end he gave up and said nothing about Kate.

He was whistling, a weight of guilt eased as he pounded down the stairs for his run, with letter in hand. The whistle died in his throat, cut off by a huge grin when he saw Kate struggling with a white lattice-work trellis. She was balancing a nail between perfectly polished long fingernails and holding the hammer delicately while trying to steady the wobbling trellis between a knee and the palm of the hand holding the nail. Presumably she planned to attach the trellis to the side of the duplex. He lounged against the rail at the bottom of the stairs, enjoying himself.

She held the nail as though it were a delicate teacup, pinched between thumb and forefinger, with the last three fingers raised, presumably to protect her manicure. The ends of her fingers shone bright pink, painted to match the cotton-candy pink top she wore over white capris.

She tapped the hammer like a true girl, and that slight movement caused the trellis to start rocking. She jiggled on one foot, trying to hold it steady with her raised knee, looking like a drunk flamingo.

"Need a hand?" he called, trying to keep the laughter out of his voice.

She jumped at the sound of his voice. "I'm not the handy type."

She held out the hammer. He took it and said kindly, "This is really a job for two people. You hold it steady."

He'd meant to save her pride, and then realized his mistake. When she stood so close to him he could smell her hair and count the nutmeg-over-cream sprinkle of freckles, he was lost.

As though she felt the intensity of his gaze, she turned to glance at him, and if he'd thought he was lost before, he was now tossed out of the universe.

Her eyes sparkled with laughter and fun, but as his gaze caught hers and held on, the laughter died and a moment of keen awareness took its place. A bird was chirping somewhere close by, and the scent of summer roses was heavy in the air. He wanted to touch her, kiss her, tell her everything. With a hiccuppy breath, she turned her head.

"The roses are so gorgeous. They're climbing roses, you know. Well, you wouldn't, because they're lying there in a heap, so this year I decided to rescue them." She was babbling he realized, and felt hope. That attraction between them had been fierce. It had also been mutual.

Maybe it was time to show her that he wanted more than friendship.

"My hero," she gushed.

He laughed back at her, noticing that she didn't pull

her hand back when their fingers inadvertently touched. Darren felt a small electric storm; she seemed to be obsessed by the side of his head.

"What? Do I have something in my hair?"

"Do your ears stick out?" she finally asked.

"I don't think so." He pulled a hunk of hair up at the side so she could see his ear.

She looked closely and then nodded as though she'd won an argument. "Just as I thought. Nice ears." She must have read the puzzlement in his face, for she laughed. "Sorry, professional curiosity." Then she looked closer. "Do you dye your hair?"

Damn it. He'd been so good about touching up his roots. He must have missed a spot.

"Yes. I went prematurely gray." He tried to smile. "We all have our vanity."

He jammed the hair back in place. He didn't want to hear anything more about haircuts, or ears, or dye or makeovers.

He knelt down and reached for one of the rose stems. The bottom was thick and gnarly with age, but lots of twiny, narrower green stems snaked around, laden with fragrant butter-colored blossoms.

The stems were also covered in thorns. He dropped his painful burden and was about to suggest they find some leather gloves when she obviously discovered the thorns herself.

"Ouch," she said, shaking her index finger as though a bee had stung it. Then held it out. "Do you see blood?"

On the pretext of bad eyesight, he took her hand in his. Her skin was so soft and smooth. He lifted her finger and could see the tiny red dot of the puncture. No blood. Lifting his gaze to hers, he pressed his lips against her fingertip. "All better," he said, unable to keep the huskiness from his tone.

She blinked, and for a second they crouched there among the roses, the sun beating down, her hand in his, the pulse in her wrist jumping beneath his fingertips. She licked her lips, and with his eyes still on hers, he leaned slowly forward.

A little gasp stopped him, and she pulled her hand away, then said, "I need gardening gloves. Twine. Shears."

"Want me to help?" he said, wondering what would have happened if she'd let him kiss her. Wondering if he was the biggest fool in the world.

"No. Thanks." She rose. "No. I'm fine." She glanced down at herself. "I should change, anyway. I'm not dressed for gardening. I saw the trellis and had to have it and then was too impulsive to wait five minutes before putting it up." She was babbling again. He decided he liked the fact that she was starting to feel flustered around him. He wasn't Dean the hopeless geek in need of a makeover. He was Darren, the hopeless geek who wanted this woman in his bed. Sure he could dress better and ditch the glasses and go back to his normal hair. But he was still the same man inside. And that's who he wanted Kate to fall for.

"Okay," he said. "I was on my way for a run anyway." And he retrieved his letter and set off, pounding the pavement with a light heart. He had a job, a life, time to work on his own programs and the challenge of wooing a beautiful woman. If the beautiful woman looked on him as anything but the "before picture" in one of those magazine makeovers, his life would be perfect.

Warm air heated his lungs as he increased his pace. He jogged past a woman in a pale blue cardigan and a plaid skirt walking a tiny black poodle. The poodle told him off sharply, in yappy little barks. The owner looked reprovingly at Darren's bare legs pumping down the quiet street. "Nice day!" he greeted the woman as he bounced past. "Humph" and "Yap, yap, yap" were the only replies.

It was a beautiful day, and not a grumpy dog or its grumpy owner were going to stop him enjoying it.

A makeover.

He grinned. One day soon he was going to let Kate make him over, but not until she saw him for the man he was inside. He wanted his princess to kiss the frog before she knew there was a prince inside.

It was a challenge. The biggest of his life.

9

SMILING AND CHATTING, blow-drying, snipping, perming and streaking, Kate made it through another long day.

They were just closing up, when the owner of the New Image salon took Ruby and Kate aside in the little storage room and slipped envelopes into their hands. "I wanted to give you a little something for your birthday, Kate, but really these are bonuses, so you get one, too, Ruby.

"We've done so well this year and you two worked harder than anyone. This is a little thank-you for all your hard work." Mona Warkentin wasn't a woman who gave compliments, or gifts, readily, so Ruby and Kate were in shock as they hugged the woman with the upswept platinum-blond hair and stumbled out of the salon.

They piled in Ruby's car and hastily tore into the envelopes. "How much did you get?" Ruby asked.

"Five hundred bucks." Kate felt the shock of the windfall. "You?"

"Same." Ruby looked as surprised as Kate.

"Wow, what are you going to do with yours?"

"The same as you." Ruby's white teeth gleamed. "Girl, we are going shopping."

And so Kate found herself at the mall, being bullied

and pushed from clothing store to clothing store and shoved into one eye-popping dress after another.

"But, Ruby, I can't afford this," she argued staring at the reflection of herself in a skimpy little skirt and tube top that left little to the imagination. She ought to put the five hundred bucks into her decimated savings account, but right now, her dreams seemed hopelessly unattainable.

"Oh, I wish I had your body," Ruby groaned. "This morning you couldn't afford it. Now you have five hundred bucks and you're not doing anything sensible with it. You are buying yourself a birthday present. A great dress." She glared at Kate before adding, "And shoes!"

"Oh, all right," Kate said, unable to resist the temptation. Maybe a shopping spree would cheer her. "This one's a little flashy, let's see what else there is." Combing through the rack, she pulled out a simple green cocktail dress. She knew the minute she tried it on it was the one. A greeny-blue silk sheath with a gauzy shawl that floated a little when she hooked it over her elbows. The dress fit where it touched, flattering her figure and allowing her hair to rule uncontested. "You like it?" she asked Ruby.

A low wolf whistle was the answer.

She turned around once more in the mirror, admiring the way the light caught the silk and turned it iridescent.

She felt good in this dress. A line echoed through her head: *Women of taste.* That's what Dean had written in the note with the silk camisole: it was what women of taste wore. So was this dress. Wearing it made Kate feel classy. It was the kind of dress you could wear with real silk lingerie and not feel like the wrong part of the outfit was on the outside.

Of course, this one classy little dress cost as much as she spent on clothing in a whole year, but Ruby was right. The money was an unexpected bonus, and what had all her scrimping and saving got her, anyway?

She took a deep breath. "I'll take it," she said to the salesclerk.

While Kate was trying not to think about how much money she was forking over, Ruby disappeared into the change room with a kaleidoscope of dresses.

Soon her friend emerged in gold lamé that appeared to be a size too small for her. "Wow!" said Kate.

An earthy chuckle escaped her friend as she strutted in front of the triple mirror. "I look like a chocolate toffee, just waiting for some lucky man to unwrap the gold foil."

"Or an expensive hooker on a Saturday night."

Another lusty chuckle. "Just see if I don't get Marvin to notice me in this." Marvin was the latest object of Ruby's lust. He worked in a music store across the street from the salon.

"And just how are you going to get Marvin to see you in this dress? Wear it to work?"

"Uh-uh. I'm asking him to a concert. One of those bands he's always yammering about is coming to town." Her smile was wide and white. "He won't be able to resist."

Kate had a superstition about clothes. An outfit was lucky or unlucky. And the trouble was you could never tell which until you'd worn the thing. Usually, if you wore a dress and had a great time, you would ever after have a great time every time you wore that particular outfit.

Unfortunately, the reverse was also true. No matter how great the clothing, if you had a lousy time the first time you wore it, it was jinxed. If she paid a lot of money for something and really wanted it to be a lucky dress, she tried to manipulate fate by wearing it to something she was almost guaranteed would be fun.

Like her birthday party. All her friends along with their significant others would be there. She lifted her chin. If she didn't have Brian hanging on her arm, she was bound to have a good time.

She and Ruby grabbed a quick dinner in the food court, giggling like kids over their new purchases. Especially over how Marvin was going to react when he saw Ruby in the gold lamé.

A pang of loneliness struck, and Kate wondered if she should wait and wear her new dress another time. Or manipulate fate a little herself.

"Who are you bringing to your birthday party?" Ruby asked her, following her thoughts nicely.

"I'm thinking of asking my upstairs neighbor."

Ruby blinked. "You haven't been getting up close and personal with those cherubs, have you?"

"No! He's a friend, that's all." But for some reason, she couldn't meet Ruby's gaze. Instead she looked for something else to snag her friend's attention and quickly found it in a coat shop off the food court. "Oh, that leather jacket would look great on you...look, the red one."

KATE WOKE TO FIND HER birthday had fallen on a gloriously sunny day. She stretched and got out of bed and padded into the kitchen to start coffee. Then she showered while it was brewing. Halfway through her first cup, the phone rang.

She lifted the receiver and held it a few inches from her ear, having an idea what was coming. "Happy birthday to you, happy birthday to you!" bellowed in her ear as her tuneless but enthusiastic younger siblings and her mother sang their greeting.

"Thanks for deafening me on my twenty-fourth birthday," she said, laughing, after they'd finished.

"Twenty-four. I can't believe you've grown so fast," sighed her mother, immediately making her feel half her age.

"And what are you planning for the big day?"

"I have to work and then I've got my party tonight. We're going out to a restaurant."

"Oh, that's grand, love. And you'll come here for your birthday dinner on Sunday."

"Yes, of course. I can't wait."

"Well, I know you've got to get off to work, so happy birthday again, darling."

"Thanks, Mom. See you then."

She hung up, smiling, and then paused as she heard someone knocking on her front door. Her bathrobe wasn't elegant, but at eight in the morning, she didn't imagine that mattered. She peeked through the door, wondering who it could be, and saw Dean.

"Hi," she said, surprised. She'd thought about inviting him tonight, but had decided against it on the grounds she didn't know him all that well and didn't want him thinking she was after a present when he found out it was her birthday.

"Happy birthday," he said, and she blinked in surprise.

"How did you know?"

"When I picked up the mail I noticed a few of those special-occasion envelopes. I held one up to the light and it was a birthday card."

She crossed her arms over her chest. "It wouldn't have said which day unless you steamed open the envelope."

"You have no faith in my powers of detection," he said with mock hurt. Then he dropped the pose and grinned down at her. "I called the salon and asked your friend Ruby."

"You called Ruby?"

"Sure, why not?"

"You don't even know her."

"I'd like to. I've heard you talk about her, and she sounds like a nice woman." He held out a brown paper bag. "Can I come in?"

"Is that what I think it is?"

"Fresh bagels. Still warm."

She opened the door wide.

"Pour coffee," she said over her shoulder as she strode for her bedroom. "I'll get dressed."

"Don't bother on my account," he said, and she laughed. Already it was turning out to be a good day.

When she got back he'd poured coffee, there were fresh bagels on a plate and cream cheese. He'd even picked up fresh-squeezed orange juice.

"You are turning out to be the best neighbor a girl ever had," she said, saluting him with her orange juice.

He didn't say anything to that, merely presented her with a small rectangular box wrapped in floral birthday paper and with a tiny mauve bow on top. With it was a card.

"Oh, Dean," she said.

He smiled and motioned her to open it.

When he'd caught sight of the topaz-and-gold earrings in the jeweler's window, Darren had immediately pictured them against her hair. He must be some kind of masochist. Now he had a new prop for his night fantasies. Kate, smiling at him, topaz glinting from her ears, swinging against that fabulous hair, while her breasts begged to be released from the silk camisole.

Her cry of delight brought him back to the present. Carefully, she removed the earrings from the small box, swinging them to and fro to watch them catch the light.

"Oh, Dean, they're beautiful." In her impetuous way, she yanked out the gold hoops she was wearing and put the new earrings on. Then she dashed to the mirror hanging in the hallway to admire them.

"I can't believe it. I love them." She danced over to him, tossing her head to make the little jewels swing. She leaned down to give him a kiss. He could tell she was aiming for his cheek, but as he moved left, she moved right, so instead of a kiss on the cheek, they ended up mouth to mouth.

He heard her sharp intake of breath when she found herself kissing him. Her lips were soft and full and tremulous against his, and the touch of that tender flesh against his mouth sparked right through him. Something lit up deep in his vitals and he had to fight all his instincts not to drag her hard against him.

With a nervous giggle, she pulled away, her color heightened and her eyes searching his with a startled expression in their depths. He gazed back into her eyes. The tiny flecks of gold sparkling in the green iris made the winking topaz seem dull.

He refused to break eye contact first. Let her see all the things he couldn't tell her. She turned to busy herself with bagels and cream cheese, while they chatted about the latest book she was reading, a runner-up for the Pulitzer, which he'd read when it first came out. In the background, the news played softly. After a bit, she said, "How'd you like to pretend to be my boyfriend at my birthday party tonight?"

"I don't know if I could ever stop," he replied. His tone was bantering, but he turned his head as he spoke and caught a gleam of interest in Kate's eyes that made his heart jump. The moment stretched as awareness flickered between them.

He smiled to let her off the hook from answering and then rose. "I'd better let you get ready for work. I'll see you later."

"Yes. Sure," she answered, still staring at him with a look of complete surprise on her face.

He was almost at the door when she said, "Dean?"

"Uh-huh?"

He watched her lick her lips, still staring at him. "Did you feel something just then?" she asked in a hushed tone.

Oh, yeah. "When?"

"When I... When you..."

"When we kissed?" he said, finishing the sentence for her.

"Yes." Her color was heightened, but her tone of stunned shock cut right through him. He'd chinked her armor, and he wasn't a man not to go after what he wanted when he sensed an opening.

"I felt this," he said, walking back toward her. He put his hands on her shoulders, gave her a moment to evade and, when she didn't, lowered his mouth to hers.

This time there was no accidental brushing of lips. He kissed her with everything he had. She was sweet and special and making him lose sleep, and he let her know it, taking her mouth with gentle persuasion and making it his.

Oh, she tasted good. Like orange juice and fresh, sweet woman. Her hair was a tangle of wet curls clinging to her back, her body slim and supple as he ran his hands down her spine.

He kissed her until she swayed against him, and he felt her hands climb his chest and link behind his neck. He kissed her until they were both breathless, and he knew he had to stop soon or neither of them were going to make it to work today.

"Happy birthday, Kate," he said at last, pulling away.

Her lips were parted and her eyes glazed. He'd like to think it was all from passion, but with an inner chuckle, he suspected it was partly shock.

"I'll see you tonight," he said, and left. She still hadn't managed to articulate a word.

"Why didn't you tell me Dean called here?" Kate demanded later that morning when she ran into the back with Ruby to grab a quick coffee between clients.

"Why didn't you tell me Angel-Butt had such a sexy voice?"

"You'd better not call him Angel-Butt at dinner tonight."

Ruby turned to her, the stir stick stopping in mid-stir. "You invited him to your party?"

She blushed. It was ridiculous. One kiss. One major steamy kiss didn't mean anything. It was her birthday, she could indulge in steamy kisses with her male friends if she wanted. "Yes. He's a nice guy, and he doesn't know many people, so be nice to him."

"The word *angel* will not pass my lips," Ruby promised with an evil smirk.

"Are you bringing Marvin?"

The evil smirk intensified. "Oh, yeah."

Kate arrived home with just enough time to shower and change. As she got out of her car, Dean came out his door and jogged down the steps with a courier envelope.

"For you," he said.

"Thanks." She looked at the envelope and not at Dean. She felt ridiculously shy after their passionate embrace in her kitchen earlier.

"Have a good day at work?"

"Yes. It was great." She glanced up at him and she could have sworn he knew damn well she was feeling shy and confused. There was an extra twinkle behind his glasses that looked suspiciously like humor.

"Can you be ready in half an hour?"

"Of course."

She took her envelope into her own suite. Who would send something to her by courier? She glanced at the shipping slip and felt sickness in the pit of her stomach.

It was from Brian.

If she were smart, she'd toss the envelope in the trash unopened, or at least leave it until tomorrow to open. She sighed. If she were smart, she never would have trusted the man in the first place. Her curiosity overcoming her common sense, and not for the first time, she opened the envelope.

Inside was a birthday card. She tapped it against her hand, then slit it open. Nothing mushy, thank goodness. It was the sort of card you'd send to an acquaintance. Or a client she thought, as she read the generic greeting on the front. She opened the card and blinked. There was a check inside. For five hundred bucks. There was also a folded, typewritten note.

Dear Kate,

I'm so sorry. What I did was wrong. I'm trying to make amends. I can't give you the money back all at once, but I'm going to send you a minimum of five hundred dollars a month, and more if I can. I'm paying you the same interest you would have got on your CD.

I got into a bad place and what I did was wrong.

I hope some day you'll be able to forgive me.

There was no closing salutation, just his name scrawled in black ink. Brian.

Well, she thought cynically, if he kept his word it would take him eighteen months to pay her back. Still, it was a start. She hoped he did keep his word, for his own sake as much as hers.

She'd closed her account with Brian's bank the Monday morning after she found out what he'd done and moved her money to a rival institution where no one but no one was getting her power of attorney.

The five hundred was a hint Brian hadn't been completely amoral. That was a start.

She showered, did her hair and makeup with a pleasant sense of anticipation. She loved parties, and when they were for her, they were extra special. She tried to tell herself, as she slipped her new earrings back into her lobes, that the exciting kiss this morning, from a most surprising source, had nothing to do with the bubbles of excitement racing through her system.

But she couldn't stop the thoughts that had teased her all day. Dean didn't kiss like an amateur, or a nerd, or a geek who loved computers more than women.

He kissed like a man who'd been put on earth to please women. She bit back a smile. A man who could kiss like that left a girl wondering what else he was good at.

When she opened her underwear drawer, she paused, and then, with a delicious thrill of excitement, walked to her closet and reached for the gift box Dean had left for her in the laundry room that day. She eased open the camisole she'd never yet worn and decided the time had come to christen the silk garment.

It felt smooth as, well, silk as she slipped it over her head and found it fit perfectly. Unable to resist a peek in the mirror, she thought Dean couldn't have chosen better. The color brought out the creaminess of her skin and didn't clash with the reddish-brown of her hair.

And it was so darned elegant, she felt like a princess. One day, she thought, she'd buy herself some panties to match. In the meantime, she slipped into a pair of beige satin-and-lace ones that sort of went with the camisole—the way a street urchin went with royalty.

With a shrug, she slipped into her new dress and heels, happy at least that her expensive new outfit didn't let down the camisole, and prepared to let the evening take its course. After all, a birthday was made for surprises.

When Dean knocked on her door right on time, she was vaguely disappointed not to be more surprised. Why, since her feelings for him seemed to have undergone a change, did she suddenly expect his appearance to alter?

It hadn't.

He looked the same. His glasses still shielded his beautiful eyes, the baseball cap still hung low, and his shoulders slouched. His shirt would make a Hawaiian sit up and take notice, but it wasn't the worst of his collection, at least. And he wore a pair of nice khaki colored slacks and decent loafers, at least.

He looked her up and down, long and slow, before saying, "Wow" in a tone that made her new dress worth every penny. "You look more beautiful than I've ever seen you."

She smiled back at him. "I thought you said you don't need those glasses all the time."

"I need them for driving," he said. Then shot her a

look that had her stomach jumping. "I'll take them off later. I promise."

Later? She didn't know about later. She'd just have to see where the evening went.

As they drove to the restaurant, she filled Dean in on everyone who'd be there and he listened intently.

"I think I've got it." He fished into his pocket when they pulled into the parking lot and out came a small black box with buttons.

"Let me just program all this into my pocket notebook. I can run into the bathroom and study if I get lost."

"You're kidding, right?" She jerked her head in the direction of the little box. "You can store notes there?"

He glanced at her in surprise. "Haven't you ever used a PDA?"

"No. Beauty consulting is pretty low tech. You don't have to go to MIT to mix perm solutions." She hated it when people made her feel stupid. For such a smart guy, Dean didn't usually make her feel ignorant.

"I don't know. You might find this useful. You could program all your appointments, track your billing, even write little memos about your clients. Like what products they like, or personal stuff about them that would make them think you really listen to them when they yack away in the chair."

"I *do* listen to them. I don't need a machine so I can pretend I'm interested in my customers. So keep your fancy gadget and your magic machine that takes the place of being a real human being. I'm perfectly happy being an ignorant hairdresser."

Even though she wouldn't look at him, she felt his eyes staring at her.

When his hand reached out to touch hers she wanted to smack it away. "I'm sorry," he said softly. "I didn't mean that the way it came out." Even through her annoyance, she felt the warmth from his hand.

She huffed out a breath. "I'm sorry. I get a little touchy sometimes when I think people are talking down to me."

"That's quite a big chip you have on your shoulder about your lack of education, isn't it?"

He was her friend and friends were honest. "Yes. I guess."

"There are different kinds of education, Kate. You've got a kind of wisdom about you that all the schooling in the world won't teach."

The way he said it she could tell he meant the words and was flattered to her toes. "Thanks."

When they arrived at the restaurant, there was a long table already set up and about half of her friends were seated. A chair with a bright pink Happy Birthday balloon floating on its own helium high, paired with a matching silver Princess balloon, made her chuckle. Her friends weren't into understatement.

She received kisses and hugs, felt herself pushed into the Happy Birthday chair and only then did she turn to introduce her date for the evening. It took her a second to find him. Dean had wedged himself into the last seat, which put him in a dimly lit corner.

As she watched, he glanced around the crowded restaurant as though searching for people he knew. Then, to her immense relief, he pulled off his baseball cap.

She introduced him around the table and he shook hands with everyone. Ruby, dragging Marvin with her, sat beside him, for which Kate was grateful. No one could be shy when Ruby was around.

10

"DID YOU have a good time?" Kate asked Dean as he drove them home.

"Yeah. I did. Your friends are a lot like you."

"Is that a good thing?"

He laughed. "It's a very good thing." He glanced over at her. "Fun, upbeat, the kind of people who make the best of things."

"Oh. That's nice."

They pulled into the driveway and the jumpiness in her stomach returned. All night they'd been exchanging glances across the table, and when they'd gone back to Ruby's place for cake he'd suddenly lost the shyness he'd exhibited at the restaurant and become easy and talkative. But the glances that were for her alone had continued.

Now that they were home, she didn't know what to do. They got out of his car and she turned to him, wishing she could see behind the lenses to his eyes, wishing he'd do something, say something. But, she realized, he was leaving the next move to her.

"Would you like to come in for coffee?" she asked, as though they hadn't already had plenty of caffeine at Ruby's place.

He put his hands on her shoulders and she experienced the same startled thrill she had this morning. "If I

n for coffee," he said, "it will be breakfast cof-
."

Her breath kind of whooshed in and out fast. "I know," she said, finally committing herself.

"Kate..." The harsh urgency of the voice spoke to her woman's heart. He pulled her to him and kissed her, hard and possessively.

"Yes. Oh, yes," she murmured back. She wrapped her arms around him and leaned in, kissing him back. After a while, her eyelids drifted open and she was staring into luminous gray eyes that told her of need and love and urgency.

She felt as though he had always been waiting for her and she for him. Her eyes locked on his, answering all the questions that had plagued her throughout the day with the inevitable answer.

"Yes," she whispered again, throwing herself back into kissing him, wanting him so badly she was rubbing her body against his in a very unsubtle invitation.

"We'd better get inside," he said on a shaky laugh, "before we break some kind of law."

She laughed back, amazed that now she'd made her decision, the butterflies had fled her stomach. No nerves now, only anticipation.

There was something about the way this man kissed her that made her think tonight would be special. Taking his hand, she led him inside her apartment and straight to her bedroom where she flipped on the bedside lamp. A pool of soft light cast a romantic glow as he turned her to him and took her mouth once again.

Excitement was beginning to build insistently. He traced his fingertips up the sides of her thighs, raising the hem of her dress as he did so, and the caress went straight through her.

Feeling cocky and in control—it was her birthday, after all—she pushed him to her bed and he obligingly fell onto his back and toed his shoes off so they plopped quietly to the carpet.

Enjoying herself, and this last present she'd be unwrapping, she climbed over top, so her knees were on either side of his thighs.

The first thing she did was carefully remove his glasses and lay them on her night table. Then she leaned forward, always watching those eyes. Her hair fell around them and he made a sound of pleasure, but obligingly didn't move. When their lips met, it was as surprising a jolt as the first kiss. She wondered if he'd always surprise her.

He lay still beneath her, following her lead as she deepened the kiss slowly, tentatively letting her tongue trace his full bottom lip from tilted corner to tilted corner before dipping inside. He groaned as her tongue touched his. She could feel the power of his restraint, as he lay quiescent, moving only his lips and tongue against hers.

Then as though unable to stop himself he raised his hands and dug them deep into her hair.

"I love your hair," he said.

Her own hands ached with the need to touch him. She reached under his shirt, dragging it upward to rub her palms over the rough hair on his chest, seeking and finding his nipples which hardened instantly. Her breasts came to taut attention in response. Dean traced the curls that framed her face. She trembled, and where she'd felt so in control a moment ago she now felt the opposite.

He caressed her slowly, his touch soft as a whisper, letting his hands roam her body, through the silk of the dress until she was so turned on she was panting, and even the thin layers of silk felt like armor.

"Sit up," he said at last, his voice gravelly with lust. She did and raised her hands, so he could ease the dress over her head.

She heard him make a tiny sound. It sounded like the word *yes*, but it was so soft it could have been a sigh. She was glad she'd chosen to wear the silk camisole she'd once thrown at him.

His eyes seemed to burn through the silk and her breasts caught the flame.

She moved to strip the camisole away but he stopped her hands.

"Leave it on," he whispered hoarsely. One of his hands came forward to touch her through the silk. His hand was not quite steady. "Do you have any idea how many times I've dreamed of seeing that camisole on you?"

While he stroked her through the silk and then slipped his hands underneath to caress her flesh, she unbuttoned his shirt, taking as much time as he had.

She opened one button, then leaned forward to touch her tongue to the part of his chest she'd exposed. She could feel the torment she was causing, and smiled at her power. When she got to the bottom of the shirt, she zipped open his slacks and began easing them off his hips.

Cherub after cherub smiled cheekily at her. She

looked up to catch the reflection of her laughter in his eyes.

"I never imagined I'd see you in these," she whispered as she removed his pants completely, leaving him naked but for the cherub bikinis.

"I couldn't stop fantasizing about you in this." He touched the camisole as he spoke, then pulled her into his arms for a kiss that left her breathless.

Still they moved slowly, treasuring each touch, each whisper. His hands were on her back, one hand sliding up the silk while the other clung to her hair.

His hungry eyes burned over her face, and when he brought his lips down on hers they were no longer gentle. His mouth plundered, demanded and received her response. He kissed every bit of her he could reach without taking off the camisole, licking and nibbling the swells of her breasts, her shoulders and her belly where the silk and her panties had parted ways, leaving a gap of flesh.

"Oh," he groaned, "I want to make love to you in this, but I want to see you." He sounded so desperate to have her, so eager that she grew hotter, enflamed by his lust which sparked her own.

His hands moved restlessly, lifting the camisole so his mouth could follow up her belly until she raised her torso once again and he slipped the garment over her head, laying it carefully aside before reaching for the aching breasts that strained toward him.

Kate gasped when he touched her, watching with a mixture of shyness and delight as his eyes devoured her. With just a fingertip he traced the contours of her breasts. Did he know he was tormenting her? Her nipples were on fire, but he ignored them and brought his mouth back to hers.

She was trembling with excitement and desire, her body a mass of needy nerve endings, each yelling to be appeased. Dean didn't kiss like a computer geek; he kissed like a seasoned professional. And she had a sneaking suspicion it was deliberate provocation on his part to have abandoned her breasts before he even got to the good part.

At last his lips left her mouth and trailed a slow wet path to her chest. He licked her breasts from the bottom up, as though they were ice-cream sundaes and he was leaving the cherry on top for last.

She was panting helplessly when he finally popped a nipple in his mouth. She grabbed the back of his head and cried out, holding him against her while his tongue did delicious things to her tender flesh. She felt a trembling begin deep inside her body and realized she was about to lose control completely.

Restless, her hands clutched at his fine-muscled back, and down over the hard round buttocks. She pulled them toward her, reveling in the hard shaft straining against the fabric of his cherub bikinis. She yanked at the waistband, dragging them down over his hips, and he pulled them the rest of the way.

He whispered, in a voice soft with reverence. "You are the most beautiful thing I have ever seen."

"So are you," she whispered back. The odd thing was that it was true. What that guy had been hiding under his geek-boarder wardrobe was a crime. His habitual slouch hid the nicest pair of shoulders she'd ever seen. Underneath those tacky shirts he'd stashed a chest fit and bronzed, abs that would have a sculptor running for marble and a chisel, while the too-big boarder shorts hung on lean hips that currently bracketed a breathtakingly impressive erection.

He took a deep breath, let his trembling finger trace the line of her temple. "Are you sure about this?" he asked, seeking the truth in her eyes.

She smiled, amazed at how right this felt. "Yes."

He nodded, and she knew the grateful relief in the smile that lit up his face. Digging into the pocket of his pants for protection, he sheathed himself in record time. So, she thought, he'd been thinking they'd end the evening the same way she had.

He slipped off her panties and lay beside her then, kissing her with passion and patience while his hands learned her body. He trailed his hands down her belly and gently opened her thighs. She cried out when he touched her.

"Now," she cried out. "Come to me now."

With fierce concentration he fitted himself against the brink of her passage, which was already beginning to throb, and grasped her hips in his hands. Then with one long thrust he entered her as she rose to meet him.

He filled her completely. She wrapped arms and legs around him, kissing him with wild abandon as they rocked together. He pushed deep inside her with each thrust, causing a timeless gasping pleasure she wanted to last forever. When she could sustain the peak no longer, she rocketed over the edge in a rainbow of light. In the echo of her own cry she heard him cry out as he thrust home one final time.

A SHAFT OF SUNSHINE poked Kate in the eye, and she realized she'd forgotten to close her bedroom curtains last night. Turning her head, she found her cheek was resting against the warm skin of Dean's chest, his heartbeat pulsing against her jaw. If she raised her head just a fraction, her lips would brush the jut of his chin.

She thought she might wake him starting with a kiss on that rather nice jaw, and fell asleep on the thought.

A lazy smile touched Kate's lips as she stretched, waking slowly. She opened her eyes to find Dean regarding her with an amused expression in his eyes.

"Hi," he said. He leaned over and kissed her briefly on the lips.

"Wow," she answered. "That was some night."

He grinned wolfishly, "Lady, you ain't seen nothing yet." He traced his hand over the outline of her breast, and of its own accord the flesh puckered and rose to meet his knowing fingers.

His touch on her body was like nothing she had ever known. She throbbed to instant life under his hands and mouth, and abandoned herself to the sensation.

It was midmorning by his watch when they finally got around to dragging themselves out of bed.

"I seem to recall you inviting me in for coffee," he reminded her.

"I did. But I didn't say I'd make it," she countered. She shook her tangled hair back, feeling well loved. "I need to shower first," she said on a yawn.

"I'd offer to wash your back, but I don't think I've got any strength left in my legs."

She laughed. "Make coffee and I am your slave."

"Done."

She stood under the rushing water, humming as she lathered her body with soap.

She emerged from the bathroom in a cloud of steam, damp curls tickling her cheeks and neck. She smiled as she watched Dean moving around the kitchen in last night's shirt—looking a whole lot better for being unbuttoned—and his pants. He was a puzzle. In some ways she felt she knew him well, and in others he was a total stranger.

He was such a good friend, she wasn't sure she was ready for them to be lovers. To trust a man so soon after the Brian horror story was probably a bad idea. And what did they have in common, anyway, a genius like him with a girl who never finished high school.

Wordlessly, she got out eggs and her frying pan.

Dean was whistling behind her as he prepared coffee, finding endless excuses to pass close enough to brush her body, each soft touch like a comforting whisper. *It will be okay.*

And she needed the reassurance. She beat the eggs until they were fluffy and lemon-colored in an effort to still her disquieting thoughts.

What was the matter with her? What had she done? She'd slept with a man she didn't know all that well, who lived right in her building, for heaven's sake. What if this thing didn't work out?

What was he thinking?

Suddenly she turned and faced him. "Dean..." Her voice came out too high. She swallowed and tried again, her eyes fixed on the Tyrolean painted bread board behind him. "Dean," she said again, more firmly this time. "I...I don't do this."

"I know," he said, a smile in his voice.

"I mean..." Suddenly things she hadn't considered last night came back to haunt her. Conversations they'd had. "I'm not casual about sex. It's not in my genetic makeup."

"I know that, too," he said, putting a hand around the back of her neck.

She tried to take comfort from him, and suddenly remembered the last time he'd comforted her, when he'd brought pizza and wine the night after Brian admitted he'd taken her money. He'd been sweet then, as well, but even as she swayed against him, certain she'd made a better choice in men this time, one comment he'd made that night stabbed at her.

He was interested in someone else. He'd told her as much. This mystery woman that he was so crazy about. Why hadn't Kate remembered her existence before throwing herself at the man?

Oh, God. She couldn't take another man lying to her. But that's what he's done, and she wouldn't hang around to be treated like a fool a second time.

She shook her head, pulling away, all the warm fuzzy feelings of a few minutes ago gone. "You lied to me," she wailed. How could she have been so stupid a second time?

Before he could say a word, she rushed out of the kitchen and went to sit on the back patio, hoping she could get herself under control before she started bawling. It was becoming too much of a habit when Dean was around.

Darren stood there for a long time feeling his euphoria drain. The smell of coffee filled the air, pungent and rich. He poured two mugs, remembered she liked hers with cream only, and carried the drinks out to where she sat gazing moodily at the fence. At least, that's what she seemed to be staring at. She certainly wasn't looking at him.

He put her coffee down with a careful click on the patio table beside her and sank to the chair he'd occupied when they ate dinner together that first time.

Her profile was set, her jaw rigid. What had happened between her getting in the shower and getting out of it? She'd called him a liar, which rankled uncomfortably. He didn't want that to be true, but had to admit it was. And yet, how could she possibly know? And what did she know? He'd been so careful.

Something didn't make sense.

He scratched his head, trying to puzzle out the sudden change in Kate. If she already knew who he was, then she must have known before they made love. So why was she looking like she was close to crying now?

Darren was a rational guy. He liked things that made sense. Mathematics, computers—he was a whiz at finding the logical answer, but women and emotions always confused him.

She picked up her coffee with a murmured word of thanks, no smile.

Bad sign.

He took a large swallow of coffee and tried to take strength from the caffeine jolt, then leaned toward her. He might as well face the music and get it over with.

"What is it, Kate?" he asked.

"Friends don't lie to each other." Her low words quavered slightly and pierced him to the heart.

"What have I lied about?" He'd see how much she knew and take it from there. That was logical. God, he was a jerk.

"Everything," she announced with a dramatic fling of her arms. "You manipulated me into falling into bed with you."

He jerked forward so fast she slopped her coffee onto her shorts, then rubbed at the spill with her finger, refusing to look at him. He took her chin in his hand and forced her head up until she was staring straight into his eyes.

He was suddenly furious. "Don't do this. You know exactly what happened last night. And you wanted it just as much as I did."

He wanted to shake some sense into the woman, but he controlled that impulse. He couldn't control his voice, however, which was getting louder as hurt and anger fueled it. "It was not a mistake," he almost shouted. "We made love last night and it was fantastic."

She wrenched her chin out of his hand, her cheeks flamed. "Oh, sure last night was wonderful, but it wasn't me you really wanted, was it?"

In corny old movies he'd often heard the hero say, "You're beautiful when you're angry," and he'd scoffed. But looking at Kate he realized it could be true. Her hair seemed to take on a life of its own when she got mad, spitting rays of molten copper and gold, and the way her cheeks flushed and her eyes sparkled—

well, the only time she'd been more gorgeous was in bed last night.

And if he didn't figure out what the hell her problem was, he had a pretty good idea he wouldn't be seeing her in bed again anytime soon.

"What the hell are you talking about?" he demanded.

"What about the mystery woman, the one you worshipped from afar? The one the makeover was for?" Her voice had risen too— She leaned toward him, her jaw at a belligerent angle. "Or did you conveniently forget about her while I was in your bed?"

A slow grin began deep inside his belly. He could feel it hit his face and he couldn't do a thing to stop it.

Kate was jealous.

She did care about him. He watched her eyes narrow until he expected her to hiss. He leaned back in his chair, enjoying the moment. He rubbed the new growth of stubble on his chin, watching her.

"Do you think it's funny?"

"I'm enjoying the moment. You see, I told you I could get her without a makeover," he said at last, not even trying to keep the smugness out of his voice.

Darren watched the emotions cross her face as his words sank in: confusion, realization and finally embarrassment. "You mean...?" Her voice was soft, tentative.

He couldn't help himself, he chuckled out loud. "That's right. *You* were the mystery woman. *You* were the one I worshipped from afar." He leaned back and stretched his arms over his head. "Ever since the moment you threw your underwear in my face I've wanted you."

Her face was flushed, her lips parted to reveal a glimpse of white teeth.

"And the more I've come to know you, the more I've wanted you," he added softly.

"Oh, Dean." He could hear the hint of tears back in her voice and he reached for her, holding her close when she threw herself into his arms. He dug his fingers into her hair, twirled a fiery ringlet on his index finger.

"I am such an idiot," she said.

"You're a darling," he corrected.

She raised her face to his. "I might make you breakfast, after all."

He kissed her slowly, savoring the soft lips that tasted of coffee.

He had to tell Kate the truth about himself. Now they'd slept together, it seemed wrong to share his naked body with her, know her in the most intimate way possible, and yet come to her with a false name and a bogus identity.

Oh, it had been fun all right to get her to fall for the geek, but he needed to share all of himself with her. He wasn't entirely sure why, except that he was pretty sure his feelings ran deeper than he was prepared to admit.

He'd tell Kate that he was really Darren Kaiser, escaped millionaire bachelor. He'd tell her soon.

But not the very first morning after they'd very first made love. Nothing was going to spoil today.

11

"I THOUGHT I was going crazy," she said after they'd had breakfast and were sitting on her couch with a last cup of coffee. Neither of them wanted to part, so they didn't.

"I mean, we're so different. You're so smart and I'm so—" She squeaked as his hand closed over her mouth.

"I hate it when you put yourself down," he said. "As well as being beautiful and kind and fun you are as intelligent as anyone I know."

She pulled his hand away and bit it softly. "Come on. I bet everyone you know has a fancy college degree," she whispered.

A lot of things were starting to make sense. The way she got all stressed out if a day went by and she didn't get a chance to read the newspaper, the way she watched educational TV and only read serious books.

He stroked her hair, took a sip of coffee. He remembered fighting with his father about which Ivy League college he'd go to—while Kate had had her chance at college taken away. The coffee tasted like ashes in his mouth.

He thought for a moment. "Why don't you go back to school? I bet you've got enough money saved to go part-time."

"It's my dream. But with a chunk of my savings gone, I'm not sure I can manage it quite yet."

"Tell me about your dream," he said, loving the sound of her voice and the contentment that filled him after enjoying the best sex of his life.

She shifted against him, snuggling her body closer to his. "I always wanted to be a teacher. Always. When we were kids I always wanted to play school." She laughed, miles away in her memories. "I had plenty of siblings to practice on, and if they got too lippy I had a couple of dolls—the perfect students."

His hands had moved around her and were comfortably settled under her breasts. She traced his hands with one of her fingers. "When the kids would learn, oh, I don't know, a new word, maybe, or get the alphabet right the first time, I'd get this feeling right here, like my heart was swelling." She touched her chest for emphasis.

He felt his own heart swelling.

She shifted uncomfortably. "I've thought about going back, but I don't know. I'd feel so stupid going to high school at twenty-four."

He grinned into her hair. "I could help you in and out of class in your walker and adjust your hearing aid."

She jabbed him in the ribs with a sharp elbow and they wrestled for a few minutes until he'd trapped her beneath him. He looked down at her, pink-cheeked, her hair spilling around her. She was laughing breathlessly.

"You'd better say yes," he warned, "before I have to resort to tickling you."

"No!" she shrieked.

"Don't say you weren't warned," he said, and, pulling up her top, began tickling her belly while she screamed with laughter wiggling crazily beneath him. Just watching her naked abdomen twist and turn beneath him was giving him ideas. He wanted her so much. Each time they made love he wanted her more.

"I mean yes," she shouted at last.

She was so beautiful, with her hair flowing out around her head, her cheeks flushed, eyes bright.

He stopped tickling but held his hands at the ready. "You mean you'll finish high school?"

"Yes." She poked her tongue at him. "And not because you are tickling me, but because it's something I have to do."

"All right."

"Is this my reward?" she asked in a breathless voice a few minutes later. One hand had sneaked up her abdomen and under her bra, where it cupped a breast. His mouth was busily trailing kisses down her throat. When she spoke he could feel the words vibrate against his lips.

With a conscious effort he raised himself off her. She'd think he was a sex maniac if he didn't turn his thoughts to something else. Trouble was, his thoughts had turned stubborn—and they were sending constant messages to another stubborn member of his anatomy with a mind all its own.

"Nope." He rose reluctantly to his feet, pulling her with him. In the distance a lawn mower buzzed, and nearby he heard birds chirping. "Your reward is that I will personally cook you dinner tonight, in the penthouse suite," he said, pointing at the ceiling.

"You cook?"

"I am a man of many surprises." More than she'd bargained for, as she'd find out as soon as they were comfortable enough with each other that he could tell her the truth.

How could he tell her now he was Darren Edgar Kaiser Jr.? She'd just started an affair with Dean Edgar, the dork who dressed like a Hawaiian Ken doll and drove the clunkmobile. If she was stressed out about the differences in their education, what would she do when she found out their socioeconomic brackets weren't quite the same, either?

She'd freak. And if he knew Kate, she'd dump him first and worry about listening to him later. Or never.

He had to move slowly, gain her wobbly confidence.

He wanted to tell Kate the truth—almost had this morning—but what she'd said about lying scared him silly. Every day he hid his true identity from her made his crime worse.

She was a woman he wanted to spend a lot more time with. She was feisty and smart and loyal and so sexy he couldn't keep his hands off her, yet underneath she was vulnerable and sweet and he found himself wanting to make life easier for her. She'd had it so damn tough all her life, and she'd made the best of things.

When he compared her life with his, he felt ashamed of himself. A thumb-sucking whiner, that's what he was. And this stupid child's prank he'd pulled could cost him the woman he was crazy about.

If he told her the truth about his identity now, she'd tell him to get lost. He knew it after what she'd said about hating lies and liars. Maybe if he just gave it a bit more time until she knew him better, then he could find a way to tell her about himself.

He felt like scum continuing with the deception, but the thought of losing Kate now, just when they'd found each other, was unthinkable. And even if she did end up telling him to take a hike, he could help her take her own life where she wanted it to go. He was beginning to see she lacked confidence in herself. She needed him to help her see how great she was.

He wanted to give her back her dreams. Whatever happened, she deserved her dreams.

THAT AFTERNOON he shopped for a meal that he knew how to cook well, and that he thought she'd enjoy. When he saw live lobsters at the market, flown in from Maine, he felt a pang of homesickness for the East Coast. His family had summered in Maine for years. Maybe it was a sly way of beginning to let her know who he really was, but he'd begin by hints and work his way up to a full-blown admission of the truth.

Nobody looked at him twice with his cap pulled low, his dark sunglasses, brown hair and the slouch that was starting to give him a permanent backache. Bart had been right. If people did look at him, it was usually one of his preposterous shirts that had snagged their attention.

Bart was smarter than he looked.

He arrived home and noticed her car was in the drive, so Kate was probably home. However, he suppressed his instinctive desire to go haul her away from whatever she was doing and make love to her.

They lived in the same building. He'd never slept

with a woman before who was geographically so very close. In fact, in his old life, he'd have automatically crossed Kate off the list of possible lovers because he wouldn't want to feel hemmed in by a woman.

Boy, had he changed. Still, he was going to have to be careful to respect her space and her privacy. They lived in the same building. It didn't mean they lived together.

So he went up to his place and started preparing dinner, forcing himself not to wonder what Kate was doing one floor below. Obviously, she was either practicing the same restraint, or not feeling the same pull to him, for he heard nothing from her until she knocked on his door at five o'clock, the appointed time for their date.

He headed for the door and noticed his glasses sitting on the table. He hesitated, then resolutely pushed them back into the plastic case and tucked them in a drawer. Maybe he could take off his disguise a little at a time, let her do her makeover.

When he answered the door, his jaw dropped. He felt the damn thing actually fall away, dragging his chin down to his navel.

He'd always thought Kate was gorgeous, but she absolutely knocked his socks off in a skimpy little halter dress that loved her body so much it clung to every curve.

"If I were a piece of clothing, I would want to be that dress," he said when he got his voice back.

"You don't think it's too short?" She glanced down. They both did, at her long, slim legs, miles of which showed beneath the short hem.

"That dress is far too short to wear anywhere else. For here, it's perfect."

She'd done her hair up on her head, with a few escapee curls around her face, and she was wearing the earrings he'd given her. He couldn't take his eyes off her. In her hand she held a bunch of summer daisies.

She was smiling at him in a way that told him she knew she'd knocked him out. She handed him the flowers. "I wasn't sure what to bring. But men never think of flowers."

He chuckled. She was right. He'd planned food, wine, even picked up a couple of new CDs he thought Kate might like. Hadn't given a thought to flowers for the table. "Thanks."

"You look pretty good yourself," she said, running her hands over his chest. "This is a new shirt."

In fact, it was a Darren shirt. One of the few items of clothing that were predisguise. Little by little he'd peel off the layers of his disguise. Ease her into the truth. It was the best idea he'd been able to come up with.

"Lady, if you want to eat, you'd better get your hands off me now," he ordered.

She pulled her hands back in mock surrender, holding them high. "Okay, I'm starving." She sniffed the air appreciatively.

"Sit down and I'll bring you some champagne."

He eased the cork out until the bottle opened with just a sigh and poured out two glasses. He'd bought antipasto at the market and bread at a trendy bakery. It had a crunchy crust and was baked with olive oil and rosemary.

He lifted his glass in a toast. "To us," he said.

She tasted the dancing liquid and her eyes widened in surprise. "Is this the real thing?" she asked.

"A lady like you deserves the best." he said.

She reached for the bottle. "Dom Pérignon. I've never even tasted it before. Oh, Dean. You mustn't waste all your money on me."

He lifted his glass at her. "It's all right, Kate. I have lots of money." Another hint dropped. The way he was going, she was going to know he was Darren Edgar Kaiser Jr. within the hour.

"Well, you won't have any money if you keep buying real French champagne."

"Isn't it great?"

"Mmm."

Soft jazz played in the background while they drank champagne, munched antipasto and talked with the easy familiarity of friends and the intimacy of lovers.

Since he had an idea Kate wasn't the type to relish boiling live lobsters—truth to tell it wasn't his favorite skill, either—he'd already done the deed and they sat, bright pink and succulent, ready to eat.

"I saw live lobsters at the market today and couldn't resist," he told her.

"Now, that's another thing I've never tried."

"Well, it's a messy business. At home my family used to summer in Maine. The best way to eat a lobster is on the beach in front of a fire. But, the second best way is right here in my apartment with lots of melted butter and a stack of napkins," he told her as he ushered her to the dinette table that looked marginally better with the blue tablecloth he had remembered to buy. Her flowers sat in the middle—a bouquet of cheerful bright yellow.

They sat, and he brought out the salad, the lobster crackers, lemon wedges and the melted butter.

Suddenly, and for the first time since he'd moved to Seattle, he missed the amenities of seduction that were a big feature of his Manhattan apartment. The killer sound system—he was making do with a ghetto blaster, the German cutlery, the Swedish wineglasses so thin and delicate he was constantly replacing them. The designer dishes a former girlfriend had picked out.

He missed his nice things, not even for himself, he decided, as he eased the cork out of a Sancerre, but for Kate, a woman he wanted to shower with the best life had to offer.

He poured wine into plebian glasses and decided it would taste just as good.

Maybe the setting left something to be desired, but the company certainly didn't. Kate was like those daisies she'd brought—colorful, cheerful and natural. For a man who'd spent his life around hothouse roses, the difference was startling and welcome.

He eased into his seat across from Kate and she looked at the perfectly cooked lobster on her plate, glanced at him and said, "Help. I have no idea how to eat this."

"Right," he said, and prepared to give his first lesson in lobster cracking. "The first thing we have to do is shield you from the mess we are about to make."

He went to the bathroom and emerged with two bath towels. "Sorry, there's no color choice. I only have blue," he said as he wrapped a towel around her neck.

"You need a safety pin to fasten it."

"Do I look like a man who has safety pins?"

She laughed. "I've got some downstairs."

"No. We'll improvise." A skill he'd enjoyed developing over the last few weeks. "Paper clips." And he dug through his stuff until he found some.

"Lobster is an aphrodisiac, you know?" he said, once she'd got the hang of digging the meat out of the claws. He watched her lick white meat from her fingers.

Her eyes gleamed with both humor and the same lust that was sparking through his body. "Are you sure it's the lobster?"

Kate laughed as Dean very deliberately pushed a plump and buttery piece of lobster between her lips, then swooped in for a quick kiss. "Oh, yeah. I'm sure."

"I thought that oysters were aphrodisiacs," she replied around the seafood. It was so delicious she wanted to moan with pleasure.

"We'll have oysters tomorrow night."

"Oh, Dean. You spoil me."

"I could spend the rest of my life spoiling you," he promised. And when she looked into his eyes, startled, she had the momentary feeling that he meant it.

They talked of nothing much. His job, her job, her friends from the party. But every time her eyes met Dean's or their hands brushed in passing, her belly would constrict with excitement. They both knew how the night would end.

Each prolonging moment was a painful teasing of the senses. Kate felt alive in every cell of her body. Her taste seemed sharper, her sense of smell more intense as she savored each different texture and flavor. Everything about the night was magical.

"I've got something special planned for dessert," he said.

"What is it?"

"You."

Her heart skipped a beat as she watched him rise and advance around the table. He leaned forward to kiss her, then, before she realized what he planned, he'd hoisted her into his arms and carried her to his bedroom.

He made short work of her dress and then laid her out on his bed.

It was the second time she'd been in his bed, she realized, and this time she was having a lot more fun.

He kissed her, dazed her with his hands and mouth and whispered promises. He kissed her everywhere, taking her up and up until she felt as plump and buttery as the lobster.

She cried out the first time when he touched her with his tongue.

She cried out again when he entered her body and took them both over the edge.

12

"HOW WAS YOUR WEEKEND?" Ruby asked.

"Fine." Kate reached under her work counter for a curling iron, letting her hair swing forward to hide her face. The women were preparing their stations before opening, sharing a hurried few minutes before customers began arriving.

Ruby perched on her chair in front of her mirror, rapidly applying makeup. "Fine," she snorted. "Angel-Butt has the worst case of unrequited love I have ever seen. And you have to live in the same building with the man. If he was Denzel Washington, well okay—but Angel-Butt?"

"Don't you think he's nice?"

"Well, sure I do. He's terrific. But what would the two of you do for fun? One of those fancy crossword puzzles? Discuss nuclear physics? Play the Mensa lovers' board game?" Ruby was enjoying her own jokes so much her lipstick was going on crooked.

"Well we could do what we did this weekend. Let's see, we ate lobster, drank champagne and... there was something else. Oh, I know. We made love endlessly," Kate told her in a husky undertone, drawing out each word, especially the last three.

"Whaah!" Ruby shrieked, jerking the lipstick in a thick crimson streak in the direction of her nose.

It was Kate's turn for unholy amusement, as she handed her friend a tissue. "Wipe your mouth, you look like the Joker from *Batman*."

"You're kidding me, right?" Ruby ignored the tissue, eyes round as saucers. She gave Kate a searching look. "Oh, my God, you're serious."

"Oh, Ruby, I'm crazy about him. He's not like I thought he was at all. He's sweet and kind and... well...I've never known anyone like him."

Seeing her friend's knowing leer, she felt her cheeks warm.

"It's not just the sex. It's him, and me...the way he makes me feel. It was just incredible."

"Honey, I have got to know, what'd he look like in nothing but angels?"

Kate thought back to the moment she'd peeled away his jeans and left him in nothing but the cherub bikinis bursting with his arousal. "He looked fantastic," she purred.

"Well, get that smile off your face, girl. Here comes your first customer." And in a louder voice Ruby called out, "Good morning, Mrs. Hodgkins. You ask about Kate's weekend, it's quite a story." And with a quick wink at Kate, who scowled at her furiously, she turned to welcome her own first customer.

While Kate cut and streaked, permed and colored, she thought about how Brian, who had seemed so right, had been so completely wrong for her. And that Dean, who'd seemed so completely wrong, could turn out to be so perfect.

Well, it was early days yet, of course, but she felt as though she were entering territory she'd never trod before. She wasn't a promiscuous woman. She gave her body only when she cared deeply. How had she come to care so deeply for Dean in a matter of weeks?

And how deeply did she care? She had the disturbing feeling that she was falling in love with the man. This time, she decided she wasn't going to be fooled by a slick appearance and ambition like Brian's. She was going to accept Dean as he was and love him for the man he was inside.

It didn't matter that his hair was awful or his clothing taste questionable, she decided. Only the man inside mattered. He was the one she was falling for. And she was falling hard and fast. She could barely wait for her shift to be over so she could get back to Dean.

However, she decided, they were going to wear themselves out if they didn't take a break from the constant sex. She shivered inside, thinking that she'd gone to sleep last night with her body still pulsing with aftershocks.

This morning, not her alarm, but Dean's tongue had woken her. She sighed. She could get used to beginning her days in such a fashion.

He'd shown her one of his favorite traditions with the lobster. Maybe she'd surprise him with one of her favorite summertime activities. A picnic.

With that in mind, she called him at home, where she knew he was still working. Soon he'd be back at his regular job and she was sort of dreading losing him so many hours to his work.

"Hi," she said when he answered.

"Hi," he said, his voice perking up when he recognized hers. "My bed felt empty when you left this morning. Do you know you make the craziest sounds right before you—"

"I think I must have the wrong number," she interrupted in the primmest tone she could manage while her body melted with heat.

He chuckled. "Don't think so. What's up?"

"I'm asking you for a date."

"Wonderful. I accept."

"You don't know what it is. Or when. You might be busy."

"I am never too busy for you."

"Also, you don't know anyone in Seattle, aren't working right now and I'm practically your only friend."

"And then there's that," he said, laughter still in his tone.

She loved how they could be so silly together, but always, underneath it was a cord that pulled them closer. It was strange, and scary and exhilarating.

"I get off work at three today. Would four be too early for dinner?"

"Right now would not be too early for dinner if it involves you."

"It involves you, me and a picnic basket."

There was a short pause. "Oh. A picnic." He didn't sound thrilled.

"What is it? You're not allergic to grass or something, are you?"

"No. I hate crowds, that's all."

Now she thought about it, apart from going to his job and out to run or shop for groceries, he barely left the house. She hadn't thought much about it, but now she wondered if he maybe had some kind of phobia.

Even when they'd been out for dinner with her friends he'd acted a little weird.

"You're not agoraphobic, are you?"

"No. No. It's fine. I'll be ready at four."

She stopped at the deli and got all the best picnic foods. Fried chicken, potato salad, some gourmet olives, crunchy bread rolls and cheese. She thought about dessert, blushed at the direction of her own thoughts, remembered they'd be out in public when they ate dinner this time, and bought some oatmeal-raisin cookies and some fruit.

She got home with enough time for a quick shower, a change into white shorts and a blue halter top, since the weather continued hot and sunny, packed her wicker basket and dug out her picnic blanket. She made lemonade and poured it in a jug. She added that to her basket along with a couple of pretty plastic glasses and some napkins. The plates and cutlery were already strapped in to the lid of the basket.

Dean looked dorkier than usual, she thought when he descended the stairs as she was packing the picnic stuff in her hatchback. She was surprised until she realized that he wasn't looking dorkier now, he'd simply made more of an effort during their weekend together. He'd barely worn his glasses once since Saturday night, and if he'd slouched she hadn't noticed. Of course, his wardrobe hadn't been much of an issue since they'd mostly been naked.

Oh, well. She remembered her self-administered lecture of earlier. He'd turned down her offer of a makeover. Obviously his appearance was a touchy subject and she'd fallen for who he was. If his outer appearance was less prepossessing, that was okay. It was the man himself who appealed to her. Not his looks.

Although, she did like his looks. She loved his serious, sexy gray eyes and the strong angles of his face. She loved his body and his smile.

He was currently wearing a ball cap for a hockey team, big dark glasses and a shirt that made her dizzy to look at. He also wore his usual too-big board shorts and clunky sandals. But he was cute in his own way.

He kissed her hello and she decided he was more than cute. He was also sexy and adorable.

"What are you smiling at?" he asked her, kissing her again so her answer was delayed.

"You. You're a true original."

She thought his grin stiffened, but as he turned away just then it was hard to be certain.

He got in the passenger side and they started off. "I know you don't like crowds, so I'm taking you to an out-of-the-way waterfront park that shouldn't be too crowded."

They ate their picnic on a grassy patch overlooking the water. After the first few minutes when Dean seemed to shrink into himself and cast wary glances around the park, he finally relaxed. Perhaps he was a shade agoraphobic and didn't realize it. She wondered if she could help him overcome his fear of crowds and open spaces. Maybe outings like this were the best thing for him.

Soon he relaxed and they ate the food, drank their

lemonade and watched the water and the other couples and the families that were enjoying a sunny evening.

She pulled out the cookies and grinned at him. "I'm sorry my dessert isn't as exciting as yours was."

When he returned her meaningful glance with interest, her shorts almost melted. Well, maybe they couldn't indulge in anything too sexual in a public park, but foreplay could take all sorts of forms.

Instead of reaching for a cookie, she plucked a bunch of red grapes from the basket and pulled off a particularly plump one.

She leaned over and slipped the grape between his lips, making sure her fingers made contact with his mouth. "When we get home," she told him in a soft, sultry voice, "you will get your real dessert."

"WHAT'S THIS?" KATE EYED the flat box, with its bright gift wrapping and gold bow, eagerly. "Another camisole?"

"Considering the last one I gave you is almost in rags, I guess I should be," Dean said, giving her a look that made her cheeks warm. "But no, guess again."

"A picture?"

He shook his head, grinning, and pushed the box toward her.

She pulled off the bow and tore at the wrapping. She'd always loved surprises, and the familiar fluttery feeling inside her stomach told her she wasn't too old to get excited about presents. She expected something intimate and sexy, and felt a warm glow deep inside as she tried to imagine what she'd find under the wrapping. Something black and lacy? Would it be transparent?

She pulled open the lid and the warm glow died. Confusion took its place. Inside the box was a flat sheaf of papers. She picked up the first one and read it over quickly.

Her heart bounded against her ribs as panic set in. "I can't believe you did this," she cried. She flicked rapidly through the rest of the papers. When she could finally speak, her voice was a husky whisper. "You registered me for school?"

"It's a special class for adults to finish high school. You start next Thursday night, but you can change it. It's up to you."

She licked dry lips, still flipping through the pages. "I was going to do it, you know. I was just kind of thinking nothing would start until the fall."

"I know." His voice was soft, full of understanding.

"Next Thursday, huh?"

"Yep. There's a summer session. If you work hard enough, you could finish high school in time to go to college next year."

"If Brian stops paying me back, I won't be able to afford it."

"You wouldn't accept my help before and I understood. But we're lovers now, Kate. Lovers help each other out. I'd lend you the money if you needed it."

She felt she could hardly breathe. Already she was nervous. One thing at a time, she told herself. First high school. Then she'd think about college. "You'll help me with my homework?"

Her dream. Maybe it didn't have to be a dream anymore. Maybe it could be reality. Maybe she'd end up continuing as a beauty consultant because she enjoyed her work and was good at it. The important thing was she'd have more options if she finished school.

"Yep."

She smiled broadly, suddenly excited. She threw her arms around Dean and kissed him. Then a sudden qualm hit her.

"What do adults wear to high school?"

KATE WAS SO NERVOUS she thought she was going to lose her supper. She crept into the classroom, hoping no one would notice her, and headed immediately for the back of the room. She sat down, her stack of new books on her lap, and glanced around. The classroom contained what looked like ordinary plastic stacking chairs, but some of the dozen or so students already there had a sort of tray thing in front of them.

Kate peered down beside her chair, and sure enough, there was her hinged desktop, hanging down the side. She reached down and tried to pull the thing up. A terrible screeching sound of metal resisting metal tore through the air. Every eye turned her way as she struggled and yanked at the tray. She got the stupid thing halfway up when it stuck, jerking Kate—and all her new books—out of the seat. The books tumbled to the floor in a series of thumps and crashes, and she followed, landing on her butt with her skirt flipped over her hips and her legs thrust in the air like a demented synchronized swimmer.

She heard a snicker from somewhere in front and felt herself grow crimson with humiliation as she scrambled to her feet. What was she doing here anyway at high school for dummies? If she couldn't figure out how to put her desk together, what hope did she have to graduate? She scrambled to her feet and was just about ready to storm out of the class forever when a quiet older man's voice at her elbow said, "They stick sometimes. Here, let me help."

Her savior was a balding man she guessed to be in his fifties. He wore blue slacks and a matching shirt with his name, Eddie, embroidered on the pocket. With two sharp tugs he had the tabletop in place and Kate sat back down with her hastily collected books.

"Thanks," she whispered to the man, who took the seat beside her.

"You're welcome," he whispered back. "My name's Eddie."

"I know," Kate smiled, pointing to his shirt pocket.

Eddie grimaced. "I got no time to change after work."

"Me, neither," she whispered back. If she'd had time to change, she would have worn jeans and borrowed an old Harvard sweatshirt she'd seen in Dean's closet, just for good luck. "I'm Kate...and I'm scared."

The older man smiled his understanding. "So was I, my first day, but it's no sweat. Just do your homework and you'll be fine."

There was a blackboard at the front of the room, and the smell of chalk dust took her back to childhood.

Then the teacher entered the room and she forgot to be scared anymore. What she felt was a stab of pure envy. The woman was probably Kate's own age, a petite blonde with a surprisingly large voice. And she was a teacher.

Kate's determination to succeed solidified as she scribbled frantically while the night school teacher outlined the curriculum and what would be expected of each student.

By the end of the two-hour class, she understood what Eddie had meant. Her progress would be entirely up to her. If she wanted to finish the year of high school she lacked in six months, she'd be doing a lot of homework. All she had to do was challenge herself a little bit and work hard.

Well, she was used to working hard, wasn't she? And this was the first step to a better education.

A bubble of excitement tickled its way through her body. She'd be grappling with subjects she hadn't thought about in years. Algebra, English composition, biology and Spanish. She could hardly wait to get started.

13

"WHAT'S ANOTHER word for *ameliorate?*" Kate asked, turning her head so her hair swung dizzily behind her. She was seated at Darren's computer, working on an essay while he prepared dinner.

Darren loved to watch her work. He loved to see her getting such a charge out of writing essays and working out algebra equations.

He stepped behind her and fed her a marinated olive, one of the spicy ones he kept in stock especially because she loved them. "Improve?"

She nodded, the crease of concentration disappearing from between her brows. "Thanks," she said, chewing.

Her eyes were glossy and full of fun and the joy of life rarely seen in anyone over the age of ten. And yet, she wasn't childlike in any way. It was more a sense that her life was an adventure.

"What?" she asked as he continued to stare at her. "Do you need the computer?"

He shook his head. He'd risen early this morning so he could get some extra hours in and worked the whole time she was at the salon. "I just like looking at you. I love this whole schoolgirl thing you've got going on. It turns me on."

She smiled and turned her head back to the screen.

"Kate?"

"Mmm?" she answered absently.

"What's another word for *turgid*?"

For answer, her right hand left the keyboard and reached behind her, where she patted the bulge in his pants as though he were an eager puppy. "*Hard*. And forget it. You'll have to wait until I finish my homework."

He loved her seriousness and her playfulness. He loved that she never complained about the fact that she was working at her regular job and then putting in hours and hours to fast-track herself to her high school diploma.

He loved her hair and her wild fashion sense, her body and the sleepy way she always licked her lips when she woke, as though she were already savoring the day.

He loved her.

With a sound halfway between a moan and a quiet sigh of acceptance, he knew that the truth had hit him and hit him hard.

He loved Kate.

He, Darren Edgar Kaiser Jr., the man who'd bolted to the other side of the country rather than face anything more serious than casual dating, had fallen in love.

With a woman who didn't know his damned name.

Love. Phew. He opened a bottle of dry white wine and poured two glasses. He set one by the side of those industriously tapping fingers, the nails flying around the keyboard like ten speeding red Corvettes as she wrote her essay.

"Thanks," she mumbled, her fingers never slowing.

He sipped his wine. Sipped again and went back to

preparing pasta and fresh seafood. All right. He was in love with the woman. It wasn't a huge surprise, it had been coming on for a while. Love. Wow.

He'd flirted with the idea of being in love once or twice before, but the feelings had passed and he remembered both those women with fondness, but no regrets. What he felt for Kate was as different as, well, as the man he was now was different from Darren Kaiser Jr.

He chopped fresh ginger and glanced at the woman who'd slipped into his heart so effortlessly.

Somehow, the give-and-take worked out. He should have totally freaked about practically living with this woman, but in fact the domestic aspect suited him perfectly. They were great together. He and Kate were a team.

Breath seemed to hesitate before entering his lungs as he faced the obvious. He couldn't love this woman and not be completely open and honest. He had to tell her the truth.

Tonight. He'd tell her tonight.

As they often did, they carried their food down to her outside patio. The sun had disappeared behind a cloud, but it was still warm enough to sit outside.

"You are such a great cook," she gushed as she bit into the halibut.

"I love cooking for you." Okay. He thought. That was a great start. He'd managed to get *I, love*, and *you* all into the same sentence. Now he simply had to get the extra words out of the way and say it again.

She blushed in that totally adorable redheaded fashion and shifted, crossing her legs. The movement had his mouth going dry. Her legs were amazing, curvy but long, and all he could think about was how they felt wrapped tight around him.

"Well, you can cook for me anytime. Tomorrow, for instance." She glanced up at him a gleam of mischief deep in her eyes.

"I would, except that tomorrow is your day off, and I have to go to SYX. Therefore, you should cook."

"Well, it won't be fancy," she said. "I need to do some studying tomorrow."

"We could go out for dinner and both have a break," he said, feeling foolishly reckless because he was in love and wanted to show off this woman to the world.

Of course, one of the best things about their current relationship was they had lots of reasons *not* to go out. Since there'd been no sightings of him recently, the media had cooled off a lot, so he felt he could go out with the woman he loved and not be spotted.

By then, she'd know the truth, anyway, if he told her tonight. He shifted on the hard plastic deck chair. He was *going* to tell her tonight.

"How about a walk after dinner?" he suggested, thinking it might be easier to talk to her if they were doing something companionable like strolling along on a summer evening. Where even if she was shocked and initially irate, he'd have time to explain.

"All right. I need to throw on a load of laundry first," she said. "Do you have anything?"

They'd taken to combining stuff to make up a load. It was a new experience to Darren to think about things like washer-load efficiency, but Kate was big on conserving water, conserving energy, conserving money.

He respected her enough to cooperat~~e~~
was something downright erotic abou~~t~~
intimate garments twisting and s~~p~~
"Sure," he said. "I've got some thing~~s.~~

After they'd done the dinner dishes, he ran upstairs
and grabbed his laundry, thinking he'd started falling
in love with her over laundry.

When he got downstairs, she was already in the laundry room, bending down and stuffing things in the
washer. Lust spiked through him as the shorts hiked up
showing a lot of slim, lightly tanned thigh, and her
nicely-rounded ass.

"Do you have anything?" she asked, her voice echoing oddly around the steel drum in the front-loading
washer.

"Oh, yeah. I've got something."

"I'm doing lights," she informed him as he advanced
on her from behind.

"There's a smudge on your white shorts," he lied.
"You should throw them in while you're washing
lights."

"There is?" she tilted her head around to look up at
him, and he said, "It's right here," gently squeezing the
middle of a firm cheek. "Best put it in the wash now,"
he continued, and while her eyes twinkled with devilry,
he slipped the shorts down her hips.

"While we're at it..." he said, then took the white
panties down as well. She gasped and a tremor ran over
her body as she stepped out of the garments and rose.

He'd give Kate credit. She wasn't slow about catching
up in the lust department. Her arms went around his

, and she kissed him as though they'd been denied ch other for months instead of hours.

"Your boarders are smudged, also," she said, looking into his eyes and nowhere near his fictitiously dirty shorts.

"They're kind of a gray color. Can they go in with the lights?" He was teasing, but sort of not. He never could figure out where the defining line was between darks and lights. Luckily for him, Kate never had any laundry angst. Especially not now.

She didn't even answer, merely reached for the fly and unbuttoned him. Off came his shorts and white briefs.

"T-shirt," she demanded, and he stripped it off and handed it to her rather than stuffing it in the washer himself. He wanted to watch her turn and bend over once more.

When she'd added his shirt, she said, "Anything else?"

"Your own shirt is very grubby."

With a grin she stripped it off, and didn't even wait for him to critique her snowy-white bra, merely removed it with gratifying haste and shoved it into the washer.

While his brain was too lust-soaked to function, she managed to figure out soap and turn the thing on so it chugged and vibrated quietly against the cement floor.

He kissed her, ran his hands down her back and over her hips, then hoisted her so she was sitting on the rocking washer.

"Aah," she gasped. "It's cold."

"I'll warm you," he promised, and parted her thighs.

The gentle vibration went all through her, he noted. Her hair trembled, catching light and glowing red and chestnut and amber. Her breasts didn't bounce so much as shudder, intriguing him until he reached forward and tasted the coral tips.

His hand slipped lower, to where she was wet and open, and already quivering in time with the washer. He helped her along with his fingers until she was doing a lot more shaking than the machine, and certainly being a lot louder about it.

With his lips still glued to a breast, he thrust two fingers inside her and that was enough to send her over the edge.

She slid bonelessly down into his arms. He caught her hips and her legs went around him to clasp tight around his waist as he eased her open body right onto his straining erection.

"Mmm," she said as he entered all that hot sweetness, which clasped him tightly.

His reply was even less coherent.

Her eyes were dazed with passion, little tremors still chasing up and down her flesh. She kissed him deep and hard, her arms wrapped around his neck, her hair floating around them both.

His climax had him staggering, holding tight to his precious burden so they didn't both fall to the ground.

Once they had their breath back, she laughed softly.

"What's so funny?"

"Unless you want to shock the neighbors, we're trapped in here until the dryer cycle's done."

"Can't have that," he said, kissing her again. "I wonder what we can find to do?"

She returned the kiss. He got the feeling they had the same idea.

Of course, by the time the washing was dry, it was too late to go for a walk.

Tomorrow, he decided, would be better, anyway.

KATE KNELT IN THE FRESHLY dug flower beds, admiring her work as she put chrysanthemums and dahlias in the small front garden so they'd have lots of color through fall. A disturbed worm twisted over on itself and began to burrow slowly back into the sun-warmed earth.

Summer was aging, she realized as she put in the flowers that would liven up her garden right through November if the weather stayed mild. What was with her and this domestic streak suddenly? She'd heard of pregnant women getting the nesting instinct—with her, falling in love seemed to bring out a domestic mania. Okay, so she wanted a permanent home with a permanent garden and a permanent man. A place where the flowers would bloom from year to year, the plants growing mature along with her love.

She and Dean hadn't declared their love for each other aloud, but it was there every time they touched, when she'd catch his gaze on her, when they fought over which DVD to rent or who was cooking dinner.

She pushed a warm curl back up off her forehead with her gloved wrist, stretching out her back at the same time in the late afternoon sunshine.

Pulling back the cuff of one red gardening glove, she glanced at her watch. If she hurried, Kate just had time to get the rest of the plants in, shower and change to get to school on time.

She smiled to herself, picturing her essay, neatly typed on Darren's computer, all ready to hand in: *Tom Sawyer and Huck Finn: A Stylistic Comparison*. She was proud of her essay, proud of her work at school and the budding certainty that she could make it into college. By then she'd have her high school diploma and enough money from what she could save and the regular payments from Brian. His second check had been for two thousand. He'd included a note telling her he was working on his problems, so that was good.

She picked up a small plastic pot and dug out a purple mum, placing it carefully into the prepared hole. The soft breeze carried the scent of the roses that had rewarded her new trellis by blooming all over the place. A low, contented buzzing told her a fat bumblebee was already checking out the mums. A feeling of pure bliss stole over her as she pressed the plant into the crumbly black earth. Everything in Kate's life seemed to be blooming.

She was in love with a man who seemed to be flowering beneath her eyes. She no longer thought of him as a computer geek. He still wore a lot of questionable clothes and insisted on keeping his terrible glasses for work, but now he was the man she loved. And whatever he looked like to the outside world, he looked wonderful to his lover.

For the first time in a long time, Kate believed she could do anything she put her mind to. When she'd brought home her first A from school, she'd walked on air.

Dean had been as excited as she was, and opened champagne to celebrate. Each step forward was easier, she discovered, because she had more confidence in herself, and because someone else believed in her. Dean was a pretty smart guy. If he thought she could fulfill her dream, it was easier to believe she could.

She was debating whether to put a red dahlia beside the purple one, or a yellow one, when she heard the car draw up. She glanced up to see a dark blue sedan purring slowly along the street, and would have turned back to her planting had the car not stopped in front of the duplex.

A heavyset man in a sports jacket stepped out of the car, squinted at the house number and back at a piece of paper in his hand, then started toward her. She didn't know why, but at the sight of him approaching, the hairs on the back of her neck began to prickle. She fought the urge to run into her suite and slam the door.

The man stopped a pace away from where she had risen to stand facing him. "Excuse me, ma'am. I'm looking for a Dean Edgar, does he live here?"

"Who are you?" Her words came out sharper than Kate intended, but something about this man filled her with dread. She didn't plan to show her worry to a strange man in an ill-fitting suit.

He pulled out his wallet. *Oh, my God, it's the police* was her first thought. *What's Dean done?*

"I'm a private investigator, ma'am," the man said.

She took the proffered card in a nerveless hand. Hank Sweeney, Private Investigator, and then some letters and addresses and more phone numbers than she'd ever seen on one small business card.

"What's this about?"

She felt like her head was full of cobwebs; nothing made sense.

"A man calling himself Dean Edgar does live here?"

"What do you mean 'calling himself Dean Edgar'?" she challenged sharply. "He *is* Dean Edgar, and yes, he lives upstairs."

"I'd like to show you a picture. Would you please identify the man as the Dean Edgar who lives at this address?"

He reached one meaty hand into an inside pocket of his blazer and Kate could see a wet patch of perspiration on the crumpled underarm of his shirt.

She took the picture in hands that shook slightly as dread settled more firmly in her stomach. She glanced down at a studio portrait of a handsome young man smiling confidently into the camera. "No," she said, almost sighing with relief. "That's not him."

"Take another look, ma'am. He could be in disguise."

Even as she opened her mouth to say the man she knew and loved would never sneak around in a disguise, the similarities between the guy in the picture and Dean began to sink in. She stared at the photo more carefully.

All at once everything fell into a pattern, like a kaleidoscope turned a certain way. Now she knew who Dean had reminded her of. Not a movie star at all. "Isn't this that missing bachelor? The one from *Matchmaker* magazine?"

"Yep."

Her eyes widened as the horrible truth began to sink in.

The hair was professionally styled, and Kate knew

the signs of a top groomer when she saw them. The style was similar to the one she'd wanted to give Dean—and which he'd refused. Somewhere inside her she registered a small note of professional pride. She'd been right, the style looked great on him.

And he was blond. Not a gray hair on his lying, cheating head. The man had dyed his hair brown to cover up its true color.

In the picture, he exuded an air of confidence. Gone was the stooping, shuffling stance she was used to; this guy knew his worth. "Cocksure," she would have called him.

Even though she could only see the upper body, it was obvious his clothes were the best. No cheap, loud shirts and oversize shorts for him. She still might have insisted the man in the picture was a stranger, had it not been for the eyes. They were Dean's gray eyes, smiling so surely back at her. The ones she loved so much.

And surprise, surprise. He wasn't wearing glasses.

"Why is he here?" she finally managed to whisper through a dry throat.

"You do recognize him?"

She nodded, unable to speak.

The man misinterpreted her reaction, for he said in a fatherly way, "Don't worry, he's not dangerous. He's just some rich young playboy from the East who left home without leaving a forwarding address. His father's had a heart attack and the family needs him to come home."

He studied her face for a moment and then moved forward to take her arm. "Honest, honey. He's not a criminal or anything. Just a cocky young fellow who thought he'd like to hide out for a while. Sit down. Can I get you a glass of water?"

She shook her head and plopped down on the stone pathway, hoping her head would clear soon.

"I thought the missing bachelor's name was Kaiser." Her voice sounded dull and tinny in her ears.

"Darren Kaiser—uh, Edgar's his middle name." She heard the satisfaction in Hank Sweeney's voice. He was obviously pleased with himself for cracking the case.

"I—I didn't really pay attention to the news stories about him, but isn't he from a wealthy family?"

The detective nodded back, winking conspiratorially. He looked the duplex over. "Guess the young lord went slumming." He scratched his ample belly. "Who can figure rich folks?"

Kate sat there staring stupidly at the brightly colored chrysanthemums still waiting to be planted.

The investigator's gaze followed hers. "They should go in before they wilt," he commented.

She was going to lose it any second. She could feel emotions welling up inside like a volcano and she knew she was going to explode any darned minute. But she certainly wasn't about to do it in front of a private investigator.

She struggled to her feet. "You'll...you'll have to excuse me, I...um...have to go out for a while."

"Sure," said her companion. "Mind if I wait? I can put the rest of the plants in for you."

"Thanks." She was already racing up the path to her door. She didn't want to be here when *Darren* returned. Didn't want to see him—not now, not ever.

Don't think about it now! she warned herself. *Just grab your car keys and go.*

Car keys.

They weren't on the little red key holder where they belonged—but then they never were. She glanced frantically round the kitchen, no sign of the keys.

She had to get out, and fast. Starting to panic now, she tore around the small apartment, willing the keys to appear.

Not in the bathroom, not in her sweater pocket.

She dumped her big leather purse upside down and a jingling cascade of items hit the floor. She hunted through loose change, rolling lipsticks, scruffy tissues, hair clips and old sales receipts. No car keys.

Her body was beginning to tremble. Where the hell were they? Without her keys she was trapped. She dashed out to the car, sneaking out the back way to avoid the detective. Not in the ignition, not on the seat or the floor...

"Excuse me, ma'am." The voice grated on her so she wanted to scream. *Don't shoot the messenger*, she reminded herself.

"Yes?" she called back.

"Are these your keys?" He was on his knees, his jacket off. In one hand he held a small trowel and in the other a dangling silver bundle.

"Oh, thank goodness."

"You left them in the dahlias."

She ran forward with a murmured thanks. When she reached him, he held out the keys and closed his fingers over her hand when she reached for them. She glanced down and saw the kindness in his eyes.

"Don't you worry, little lady," he said gently. "Everything will work out. He's probably got a good explanation."

His ugly-kind face blurred before her eyes. "How did you know?" she whispered.

He chuckled softly. "I'm a detective, remember? Figuring things out is what I do. And if I couldn't figure out you're in love with this fellow after all the clues you've been throwing my way, well, I wouldn't be much of a detective, would I?"

She gave a shaky laugh. "I guess not. It's such a shock. I've just got to get out of here before he gets back. I...I can't see him right now."

"Sure." He hesitated, still holding her hand. "You okay to drive?"

"Uh-huh."

He appeared doubtful, so she forced a smile. "I'm not going far."

"My guess is you're too good for him, anyway." He squeezed her hand before letting it go.

"Right again, Detective," she said, and, turning with a wave, ran lightly back to her car.

Not until she was sitting in Ruby's living room did she finally let the lava overflow. And when it did, she thought it would never stop—burning molten liquid scorched twin paths down her cheeks. Her eyes were burning, her head, her stomach.

"I thought he loved me," she wailed into a damp tissue, one of about two hundred little wet balls that surrounded her. On her lap sat an empty box of tissues, and an unopened one sat ready at her side.

"Hey, now. You don't know he doesn't," Ruby said, her face wrinkled with worry.

"But he lied to me, Ruby. His whole life with me was n-nothing but a l-lie."

"All I know is I'd like to shove those damn fake glasses of his down his pencil neck." Ruby said savagely, making a jabbing motion with her hand. She re-filled their empty wineglasses and drank deeply.

Kate pulled another tissue from the pack. Her cheeks were beginning to chap, she'd been crying so long.

"And as for that computer—well, I know where I'd shove that."

It was after midnight when Kate pulled into the driveway of the duplex. She heaved a sigh of relief. The place looked deserted.

It wasn't until she was almost at her door that she spotted him, sitting on the dark step, waiting.

"You've got no business here, Mr. Kaiser," she said coldly.

He rose stiffly, as though he'd been sitting on the outside step a long time. He had a key to her place, but he hadn't let himself in. Perversely, that annoyed Kate as much as if he'd assumed the right to wait inside.

"I have to talk to you."

She thought she'd cried every tear out, but the naked appeal in his voice brought another lump to her throat. Her swollen eyes ached with emotion.

"More lies? I don't think so."

"Look, I was afraid to tell you the truth. Afraid to lose you. I love you, Kate."

He finally said those words she'd longed to hear, and

now she wanted to throw them back in his face. "How do I know that's not another lie?"

Her eyes were becoming used to the dim light, and she could see he was wearing different clothes, which hung perfectly on his tall, straight physique. Already he was a stranger.

She wanted to cry for the sweet, kind of hopeless nerd she'd come to love. The one who didn't really exist. She hated this perfectly turned-out celebrity-on-the-run for robbing her of Dean.

"Please, Kate. I have to go back home. My dad's sick. I couldn't leave without seeing you."

"So you've seen me. Now, if you ever felt anything for me, leave me alone." The quiver in her voice infuriated her so much she shoved the key into the lock, yanked the door open and walked in without a backward glance.

"Kate, please...I tried so many times to give you hints, and every time I got close to telling you, I guess I chickened out. Nothing in my life has ever meant as much to me as the time I've spent out here with you. I didn't mean to get close to you, I never meant to hurt you and I sure never meant to fall in love with you, but it happened."

She turned on him, fury almost choking her.

"You've had your fun hanging around with poor people and losers, now get the hell back to where you belong and stay away from me. How could you do this? I feel like the dupe in one of those reality shows. Only I never signed on for a TV show. I only wanted to live my life." She sniffed and stared into the face she'd believed she could trust. Once again she'd been made a fool of, but this, she knew, was going to hurt so much more than the Brian fiasco. "All I've ever wanted is honesty."

She didn't slam the door, she simply closed it quietly in his face, shutting him out of her life forever.

14

DARREN'S FOOTSTEPS echoed eerily down the endless maze of hospital corridors until he entered the intensive care unit; there the floors were carpeted. It reminded him of a library, everybody trying so hard to be quiet.

His steps slowed as he approached the nurses' station.

He suddenly felt he wasn't ready to see his father. His collar was choking him—how long had it been since he'd worn a tie? He did so now out of respect, but it felt as foreign to him as those stupid glasses had a few months ago.

A smiling nurse gave him directions and warned him not to stay long. And then suddenly he was there in the doorway looking down at his father.

A lump formed in his throat. It was all wrong to see his powerful father lying there looking so vulnerable in a pale blue hospital gown, tubes snaking everywhere from his body to countless blinking, burbling machines.

He was the only patient in the room, but it seemed to be walled completely in glass, so privacy was an illusion at best. Darren knew the nurses were monitoring his father constantly, but still, the lack of privacy irked him.

His father regarded him with eyes that were restless and alert in the gray, slack skin of his face.

"Hello, Dad," Darren said at last.

"So, I almost have to kick the bucket to see my own son."

"Aw, Dad, I'm sorry." His voice sounded husky. He cleared his throat and tried again. "How are you feeling?"

"How do you think I feel? I've got goddamn tubes up every orifice, and they punched in a few new holes just to put in some extra wiring."

Darren smiled slightly. This was more like his dad. He sat in the plastic chair angled near the bed.

His father turned his head to face him. "Even that useless lawyer of yours, Bart, couldn't find you quickly. Your mother's been going crazy."

"I never thought you'd need me." Darren looked down at his hands clenched together in his lap. "I just had to get away and see if I could do something on my own."

"Hmm. And did you?"

Darren nodded, glancing warily up at his father.

"Well, what is it? Tell me quick before I have another heart attack."

"Computers. I've almost finished the special education software program I was working on."

"Goddamn computers," the older man muttered.

Darren shrugged. "This is what I spent all my spare time on in Seattle. The program needs testing, of course, but I think it could have a significant impact on teaching struggling readers."

His father regarded him through narrowed eyes. "So

you did something useful, then? I suppose this means you're not coming back to KIM?"

Darren was watching his father carefully. His Dad was quiet but for the buzz and whir of machinery. He breathed in the antiseptic smell and waited.

He did not want to be having this conversation right now. Darren was terrified his father would fly into one of his anti-computer rages and set off all the machines clanging and banging and flashing all over the ICU.

"I had to make my own path, Dad."

To his surprise, a slow grin spread across his father's face. "Me, I went to New York."

"What?" Darren felt his eyes widen. He'd expected a tongue-lashing and he was getting smiles.

"I was younger than you, and I guess I thought my old man was as much of a stick-in-the-mud as you think I am. So I left our home in Pittsburgh. Your grandfather had a deli business he wanted me to inherit, but I wanted to wear a suit and drive a fancy car. I moved to New York, started on the bottom rung as an ad copywriter. Well," he said with a wheezy chuckle. "You know the story from there."

He turned a fierce eye on Darren and picked up a hand to shake a finger at him, flapping the intravenous tubes like skipping ropes. "But I respected my father and the things he talked to me about, like working hard and giving good value to the customer, even though I thought he was an old stick and he thought I was a cocky young know-it-all."

Darren shifted uncomfortably in the hard chair, which seemed designed to encourage visitors to keep their visiting to a minimum. "Point taken."

There was a pause that magnified the blips and gurgles of the monitors. "Mary Jane Lancer got engaged to Larry Norbert."

Darren couldn't believe it. He snorted with laughter. "She's going to marry Larry? The tennis pro?"

"He's a junior banker now in her father's firm." His father's voice crackled with disapproval.

"Huh, what do you know?" He breathed deeply, wondering if his father could take any more. "I, um...I have something else to tell you, Dad."

"From the look on your face I'd say it's going to cost me big."

"No! No! It's just that I met a woman in Seattle." He dropped his head into his hands. "Oh, God, Dad, I made a mess of everything."

"Some little gold digger get her claws into you?"

"No!" Darren felt anger rising. "She doesn't know who I am. I mean, she didn't. Now she knows, she threw me over."

It was his father's turn to be outraged. "What do you mean she threw over a Kaiser of Kaiser Image Makers? Does she have any idea of your net worth?"

Darren chuckled softly. "I doubt it. She loved me when I was a struggling computer nerd, now she knows I'm the Match of the Year, she thinks I'm a jerk."

His father looked suspicious, eyes narrowed. "She's not touched in the head, is she, son?"

"No, Dad." He thought for a moment. "You know, you'd like her. She's straight-talking, she has a hot temper, and she's so pretty it hurts to look at her."

"And you let her get away?"

"I told you, she dumped me when she found out I'm a rich guy."

Darren Kaiser Sr. sighed loudly, raising his gaze to the ceiling. "Women!"

A smiling nurse appeared, a small tray in her hands. "Time for your medicine, Mr. Kaiser, and I think this young man has taken up enough of your time for today." Her smile was still wide but her tone was clear. It was time to go.

He and his father exchanged a glance, which said, as clearly as his father just had, "Women!"

Darren moved to the bed and held out his hand. His father shook it. The clasp wasn't as firm as usual, but it was there.

"I'll be back tomorrow, Dad. Take it easy."

"You, too, son." His father was smiling as Darren left.

KATE KNEW DARREN WAS GONE the minute she returned home to the duplex after work. She felt his absence. It was like a physical ache, knowing he had betrayed her and then left.

She glanced around, half expecting to see a letter addressed to her, which her fingers itched to tear up, unread—but there wasn't one. She found her key, though, in the middle of the dining table. He hadn't even taken it off the silly plastic key ring she'd given him. Just seeing the white plastic computer shape with the red printing, Computer Programmers Do It with Bytes brought an ache of longing.

She waited for flowers with a "let's make up" note, but none were delivered. Too bad, the old folks home was probably ready for some new blooms.

She had expected the first night after he left to be the worst, and it was. She worked doggedly on her homework, determined to make up for the class she'd missed while she was crying her heart out at Ruby's. She was just as determined to put Darren Edgar Kaiser Jr. out of her mind. But he kept coming back, like the twin specters of Dr. Jekyll and Mr. Hyde she was writing about for her next essay.

Dean Edgar was gone. Had never, in fact, existed. But his loss was like the death of a loved one. For she had loved him, and he would never come back.

Darren Kaiser was the kind of uptown guy who looked down his nose at girls like Kate. All his girlfriends probably had hyphenated last names, and a different purse and shoes to match each designer outfit.

Kate swore as she scratched out yet another wrong answer to a simple math problem.

So he'd come to Seattle slumming. He was probably having a few martinis down at some absurdly exclusive rich boys' club with his friends about now, laughing about his adventures in Seattle. And the girl he'd made a fool of.

Her teeth ground together; the pencil snapped in her hand. With a cry of frustration she threw the pencil pieces across the room and took herself out for a punishing walk. She had to keep busy or she'd drive herself crazy.

She took on extra shifts at work, and every spare minute she had, Kate worked on her high school diploma. She was more determined than ever to succeed. And if, at the end of working a double shift and spending several hours plodding through algebra problems, or writing compound complex sentences, she went to bed only to lie wide eyed and aching with a pain that wouldn't ease, then no one had to know about it.

Ruby did her best to be a great friend, forcing her out to a movie one night, but unfortunately it turned out to be a bittersweet love story that left Kate sobbing.

She refused to answer her phone, and a couple of times she stood over the ringing telephone, knowing with some sixth sense that it was Darren at the other end. She turned on her heel and left the apartment before she weakened, the phone still echoing in her ears as she reached the road.

After several weeks the pain hadn't lessened. If anything, it was getting worse.

"You look terrible," Ruby said to her over a cappuccino at Starbucks.

"Thanks." Kate stirred the coffee vigorously until the foam looked like whitewater rapids.

"What are you trying to prove, girl? Working your tail off, pulling in straight A's at that foolish school of yours, and for what? To pretend Angel-Butt didn't break your heart?"

Kate had spilled some sugar on the table; now she was engrossed in drawing patterns in it. But at this she looked up into the accusing eyes of her friend.

"Well, he did break your heart. So get over it. Get a life!"

"I'm trying, Ruby. It's just so hard," she said, choking on the words.

"No, you are not trying. You are wallowing in self-pity. How many letters have you got from him?"

"None." Kate jabbed the air with her index finger.

"What! You telling me you dumped a guy and he doesn't even have the decency to grovel?"

"Well, he sent me eight letters so far, but I tore them all up before I read them," Kate admitted.

"Well, all right. That's better.... Phone calls?"

Kate flicked her hair back over her shoulders. "I don't answer my phone, and I unplugged my answering machine."

"Ooh, you've got it bad." Ruby sat back and crossed her arms. "You're going to have to move."

"Move?" Kate was stunned.

"Sure. That place is full of memories. Every time the phone rings you think it's him. Every time the mail arrives you check to see if there's a letter or a card from Angel-Butt just so you can tear it up. You gotta get out of there before you end up as Mrs. Butt."

"Not hardly. Didn't you see *Darren* on *Entertainment Tonight?*"

"Damn, I was hoping you'd missed it. I never would have recognized him."

There'd been a short feature about the return of the Match of the Year, but the report had focused on Darren's father and his brush with death, how his devoted son had rushed back to his father's side. When pressed as to what he'd been doing all this time, Darren had merely said, "I was pursuing some personal interests."

Kate had almost broken her television remote control when she jabbed the off button. He'd found time for a haircut and his color was back to golden-boy blond. He'd worn casual clothes, but not the garish shirts and board shorts she'd grown to like. No. He could play a round of golf in Beverly Hills in these casual clothes.

Unlike Ruby, she'd have recognized him anywhere.

She had to get him out of her mind, out of her heart and out of her dreams. Moving was so logical, Kate couldn't believe she hadn't thought of it herself.

"You're right. A new start, that's what I need. I should find a cheaper place, anyway. Maybe I can get something closer to the university." Since she'd be cutting back on her hours at the salon to attend classes in the fall, it made perfect sense.

"And far from bad memories."

"Ruby, you are a genius." She raised her cappuccino cup in a mock toast, forcing cheer into her voice. "To a new beginning."

Once she'd decided on her course of action, Kate wasted no time. She gave notice on her apartment and started concentrating on her new life while she tried to put the old one behind her.

When the telegram arrived, Kate had her head under the kitchen sink packing up the cleaning supplies. She answered the door, debating whether to keep the bug spray or, since she was too much of a softy ever to spray bugs, anyway, to throw the stuff out.

"Is your phone out of order, miss?" the uniformed messenger asked. "We've been trying to get you."

The phone had been ringing every hour, spurring Kate's cleaning and packing efforts. She blushed. "Oh, I've been busy, sorry."

Telegrams delivered at the door always reminded her of war movies when the little square of paper said somebody wasn't coming home from battle. Maybe that's why she just signed the receipt book before checking who it was from. She shut the door and tore open the telegram with anxious hands.

Kate:
  Arrive Seattle tonight. Must see you.

  Darren.

"Damn you, Darren Edgar Kaiser," she shouted at the paper in her hands, then tore it into pieces over and over again until it looked like confetti all over the floor.

She uncapped the lethal bug destroyer and sprayed the little pieces of paper with a vicious hissing until she was coughing in a cloud of noxious fumes.

She grabbed the phone and dialed. "Ruby, Darren's coming back tonight. Can I stay at your place for a couple of days?"

"Don't you think you should at least see him?"

The bug spray was on the kitchen counter, pictures of scaly lifeless corpses on a satisfyingly bloodthirsty red background. "If I see him I'll end up arrested for murder. You've got to help me out."

"Sure, honey. Come on over. We'll have a Friday night pizza and rent a movie. Sound good?"

THE SALON WAS BUSY with the usual Saturday rush.

Kate and Ruby worked side by side perming, coloring, curling, snipping, exchanging a few brief words in passing.

In defiance of her low spirits, Kate was brightly dressed in an electric-blue cotton miniskirt and a blue-and-fluorescent-green floral sleeveless top.

It was about midday and she was between clients when she noticed a run in her panty hose and dashed into the supply room to change into a fresh pair. She had the old pair off and the new one pulled up to her knees when the receptionist ran in.

"Oh, there you are, Kate. You've got a new customer and he's a hottie. I put him in your chair already." The girl tried to leave but Kate grabbed her by the arm.

"Wait," she squeaked, dragging the girl back into the small room. She dove behind the door and peeked out through the crack.

Just as she'd suspected. It was Darren. Sitting there, in her chair, just like he had a right to be there.

"Ow, you're hurting my arm! What's going on?" the girl cried out from behind her.

"Get Ruby. Send her in here."

"But she's just going off on her lunch break."

"Do it!" Kate turned savagely on the young receptionist, who stepped back hastily when she saw Kate's face.

"All right. Be cool."

The girl sped out of the room.

Kate remained crouched behind the door, eyes narrowed to slits, glaring out at Darren.

He was sitting at ease in her chair, looking around with interest at the salon.

She wanted to use her hot curling iron like a cattle prod and eject him out of her chair. The nerve of him, coming into her salon and sitting in her chair, just as though he hadn't lied to her and broken her heart.

How dare he?

She didn't see Ruby coming until the door flew open.

She squealed with pain and fell back onto the floor, holding her throbbing nose.

"What is going on?" Ruby hissed. "Sally thinks you're having a fit of some kind."

"It's hib." Kate gestured with one hand, the other still clapped to her nose. "Id by chair."

Ruby stared out the door, a slow smile warming her face. "Angel-Butt went and got himself gorgeous."

"He's evil." Her nose felt like it was swollen. "I think I broke by dose."

Ruby peered down at her, still crouched on the floor. "No, you didn't," she said kindly. "If you'd broken it you'd be bleeding all over the place like a stuck pig."

"You have to do him, Ruby. I'll sneak out the back."

Her friend glanced out the door again and then back. She shook her head. "He's your customer, and that's your chair."

"I can't, Ruby, I can't." Surely the tears that welled in her eyes were due to her injured nose. She sniffed loudly, prodding gingerly to see how badly swollen it was.

"Honey, it's time to stop running and hiding. You're a big girl. If you don't want him, tell him to his handsome face." She put her hands on her hips. "And then put him in my chair."

Kate's chest felt like an elephant was standing on it. "I'm scared," she whispered.

"Look, you're on your turf, with your friends and customers all around you. What can he do? Be a grownup and get it over with." She held out a hand to help Kate up.

She struggled to her feet and pushed her hair back

over her shoulders. "You're right. I can't wait to take my scissors to him." She reached for the doorknob.

"Honey?"

She turned back to Ruby, her brows lifted.

"You'll make a better impression if you pull up your panty hose first."

THEIR EYES MET IN THE mirror. She saw emotion blaze in his and then it was gone.

"Hello, Kate." That deep rich voice that had once whispered endearments and promises to her was steady.

She licked dry lips, willing her heart to slow down. "What do you want?"

I want you back his eyes said. "A haircut," he said out loud. He'd already had at least one since she'd last seen him. He wore a burgundy golf shirt with an insignia on the pocket and perfectly pressed taupe pants. He resembled the man in the picture the private detective had shown her.

"Last time I offered you a haircut you turned me down."

"I changed my mind."

She was determined to hang on to her professional demeanor in spite of the hurt and anger that threatened to overwhelm her. She picked up a comb and ran it through his hair. The thick strands brushed her fingers and brought back memories of all the times she had run her fingers through his hair in play and passion. Of course, it had been brown in those days. Just part of the false veneer.

Their eyes met again in the mirror.

He felt it, too, she could tell. Then, as he scanned her face, a frown appeared between his lying, 20/20 eyes.

"What happened to your nose?" he asked.

She flushed uncomfortably. "I banged into a door," she said stiffly.

"How are you?"

"I'm fine. Never been better." Lies, lies, lies.

She wasn't going to tell him about her own life. She'd chatter all that inconsequential stuff she managed all day long. Except she couldn't think of a single inane thing to say.

Instead, she babbled the first thing that came to mind.

"Brian has a new girlfriend. A woman he met at AA. He came by the salon last week to apologize to me. I guess he's getting himself straightened out."

"Did he give you the rest of your money back?"

She nodded. "He sold his car."

"It's one of those steps they have to take in the program. Right old wrongs and stuff. His girlfriend was with him. She'll be good for him; she's tough, she'll keep him in line."

Darren settled back in his seat. "Good."

"Come on," she said. "Let's get you shampooed."

Of course, the shampoo girl already had one wet head in her sink and another customer waiting. If she stuck Darren in the line, he'd be in the salon that much longer. She just wanted him out of her chair and out of her life as soon as possible, which meant shampooing him herself.

She sat him down, stuck his head in the sink and tried to remember which shampoo smelled the worst.

She worked the lather through his hair, massaging

his scalp just as she would with any customer. Never had a simple shampoo been so difficult. She was forced to bend over him, knowing her breasts were just inches from his face. She felt herself responding to his nearness, while she felt him looking at her, breathing beneath her, and she wanted to hurt him. And she wanted to kiss him.

She rinsed the shampoo out of his hair and wrapped a clean towel round his head, giving it a brisk rub, then led him back to her station.

She combed his wet hair and made a production of preparing her scissors and combs on the tray in front of her. Then she took a deep breath and picked up a comb and scissors, and began trimming his hair.

"Kate, I started to tell you who I was about twenty times, but I always got scared. I thought I'd lose you." His voice was low and intense. She forced herself to concentrate on his hair so she wouldn't weaken and gaze longingly into the gray eyes reflected in the mirror.

His hair grated against the sharp blades of the scissors as she cut through it. "You were right," she said coldly.

"You thought I was lying, but I wasn't. That guy you knew is me as well."

Snip, snip.

"God, I don't even know who I am anymore. The time I spent in Seattle was more real to me than my other life. It's so easy to get trapped into what other people think we should be. How we should act, how we should look, who we should be with. It takes courage to change."

"Or some hair dye and a handy discount store."

"I was a coward, I ran away because I was turning into something I didn't want to be. Can you see that? I was always That Darren Kaiser, who was only a vice president of Kaiser Image Makers because his father built the company. I wanted to know if I could do anything else but be That Darren Kaiser. The *Matchmaker* magazine was the kick in the ass I needed. It gave me the perfect excuse to follow my own path, and I found out I could be the real me."

He raised his head to search her face in the mirror. "And I found you."

"Stop moving your head, please." She meant it to sound sharp and professional, but her voice wavered. He'd be served right if she gave him a buzz cut that would take months to grow out.

"I was so busy thinking about myself, I never thought about what this might do to you. Right from the beginning I tried to stay miles away from you, make sure you didn't want to know me. But I was lost from the minute I saw you."

"Bend forward." She moved behind him, pushing his head forward with unnecessary force. She heard his chin strike his chest.

"I'm not asking you to take me back." His voice was muffled against his chest. "I just want you to give this new guy a try. Get to know me. I'm miserable without you. And you look pretty miserable, too."

"Well, I'm not. I'm tired from studying." She paused. "I start college in the fall."

His head flew up, almost knocking the scissors out of her hand. "Kate, that's great." He beamed at her.

"Come on. Let me take you out to dinner tonight, to celebrate. As friends, no more."

She bit on her lower lip, considering.

She couldn't keep tearing up letters, dodging telegrams and moving. Maybe she should just have dinner with him, make it clear it could never work between them. Say goodbye with class. He didn't deserve it, but *she* did.

Tapping a comb against one palm, she said slowly, "I'm staying at Ruby's. You'll have to pick me up there."

He grinned at her. "Deal."

15

KATE PACED up and down Ruby's small apartment. "Do you think this dress is too short?" she asked anxiously.

"You've already changed three times," Ruby answered in exasperation. "The man knows you've got legs, forget about it."

She had settled on the green dress she'd worn to her birthday dinner. It brought back painful memories, but it was the best thing she owned to wear to a fancy restaurant.

"Does my nose still look swollen?" She touched the tender spot where she'd applied an extra coat of foundation to cover the redness.

"You look gorgeous."

They heard a car approaching. He was right on time. Kate turned to her friend in panic. "Oh, God, Ruby, I'm going to throw up."

"No you're not. You are not going to the best restaurant in town smelling like vomit. Breathe." Ruby stood up and demonstrated, waving her arm theatrically: "In—one, two, three. Out—one, two, three. In—one, two, three…" The doorbell pealed and she moved to answer the door. "Out—one, two, three."

"In—one, two, three," Kate gasped. "Out—one, two, three."

She was panting like a thirsty dog on a hot day.

She heard Ruby and Darren at the door making wary chitchat.

In—onetwothree. Gasp.

She stumbled forward.

And forgot to breathe at all.

Darren was standing there—and so was Dean. His lightweight navy suit was superbly cut. That was definitely Kaiser, as were the rest of the clothes, shoes and posture. But the face belonged to her Dean, and his hair was her creation.

When she looked into his eyes, she knew him. The expression was warm as those gray eyes looked back at her, but he treated her like an old friend. No kiss or touch, just a "Hi" and then they were off.

"Where's your car?" Kate asked, looking for the old clunkmobile.

"Here," he said, gesturing to a late-model Ford. "It's a rental. I flew in last night."

Of course he wouldn't drive the beater anymore. He'd gone back to his old life. She had to remember that. But then why was he here with her? What part could she possibly play in the life of Darren Kaiser of Kaiser Image Makers?

Her feeling of disorientation continued as they walked through the crowded restaurant to a window table. She could see women's heads turning to look at Darren. It had never happened before when she'd been with him and she didn't like the twinge of possessiveness she felt.

Finally they were seated and she was sipping a glass of wine while Darren swirled a Scotch on the rocks.

"How is your father?" she asked politely.

"He's home now and out of danger." He put the drink down with a dull thud on the white tablecloth, causing amber liquid to splash out of the glass. "I was a jackass to go like that and make it so hard for them to find me. He could be dead now."

Of all the feelings she'd expected to experience in his company, this sudden surge of empathy and remembered pain were a surprise. She nodded, knowing exactly what he was going through.

"You always feel guilty—and angry—when they die." She drew a little pattern on the white cloth with her fingernail. "My dad promised me he'd dance with me at my high school prom. He promised me I could be anything I wanted to be when I grew up."

Her voice was growing husky. She paused, swallowing. She remembered the rage she'd felt after her father's death. It had shocked her, and made her feel guilty.

She remembered the bitter reality. Prom season was a busy time at the beauty salon, and every year it came around, Kate felt like Cinderella dressing her stepsisters for the ball she couldn't attend.

"He lied to me," she whispered at last. "He didn't mean to, but he lied. It seems a habit with the men in my life."

She dipped her head to her glass, blinking the sudden moisture away.

"Kate, I never lied to you."

"Your whole life here was a lie."

"No! You saw the real me. Oh, not the phony glasses and those insane shirts, but the guy who shoots straight to the moon every time he gets his hands on a computer. That's more me than a desk in an advertising agency."

She gave a noncommittal grunt.

"I'm also the guy who loves you. All the time we spent together, all the hours we made love...damn it, didn't that tell you anything?"

"Dea—Darren, please..."

"Okay, so I look a little more presentable and have a few bucks, is that so terrible?" He waved a hovering waiter away with a quick gesture, holding Kate's eyes with his own.

"I don't see why you didn't just go off and do a computer thing as the real you." She leaned forward.

"It was knowing that if I did I could always run to my dad if I got in trouble. That if I tried to get a loan, I wouldn't know if I got it on my own merits or because my dad plays golf every week with the bank manager. Coming out here gave me a clean start, and whatever I did I would do on my own. It probably sounds nuts to you. It sounds nuts to me now, but at the time, I had to do it. That's all."

"You should have told me." Her voice vibrated with pain.

"And have you run away even sooner? Everything's a risk, Kate. And love's the biggest risk of all—I love you, and I'm willing to do whatever it takes to give us a another try. How about you? Are you too scared to take a chance?"

All through dinner, when she ate delicacy after delicacy, which all tasted like sawdust, and drank expensive wine that could have been tap water, she tried to avoid answering his question. Darren must have realized he'd given her enough to think about, for he backed off and asked about school, her family and her plans for the future.

Just as he'd promised, he drove her back to Ruby's apartment before midnight. He didn't even suggest taking her back to his hotel room.

She was relieved. Of course, she was relieved.

Darren turned to her. In the glow of the streetlight his face was vague, so she had to rely on his voice and eyes, both so very familiar to her.

"Kate, I have to go back East in a few days. Dad needs me at KIM for a while. I can't let him down again."

Her heart sank. So he thought she didn't need him? "I understand."

"Come with me," he said.

"Are you crazy?"

"You could go to university in the East. There are some great schools."

"And you or your Dad would pull some strings?" She couldn't keep the scorn out of her voice.

He chuckled softly. "Now you know how I felt. No, you have the marks to get into a good school all by yourself."

"You're asking me to leave everything I know and move to the other side of the country for you. To do that, I'd have to trust you, and I can't."

"You know, one advantage to being That Darren Kaiser is that I can afford to make things easier for you and your family. You could come home and visit whenever you want, in time we could help your mother find a better place to—"

"How dare you?" she lashed out in blind fury. "We've never had to turn to charity yet, Darren, and I sure as hell won't take it from you."

He reached for her hand, forcing the connection between them she didn't want to feel. "Forget about all the surface stuff. Trust your heart. In your heart you know me."

She felt as fluttery as a trapped moth. "I don't know you...I don't."

"Trust this," he said, and, leaning forward, cupped her face in his hands and kissed her. She made a little moaning sound of despair in the back of her throat as her body leaned in closer to his embrace. She could feel his life force flowing through her, and her answering response flow back to him.

He pulled away at last, and she felt bereft without his warmth.

He got out of the car and walked around to Kate's side to open her car door. He walked her up the path to Ruby's door. "Sleep on it," he said. "I'll call you tomorrow."

The door opened to reveal Ruby in a crimson bathrobe, a towel wound into a turban around her head. Before Kate could reply, he had waved to both women and was walking back to his car.

Sleep on it, he'd said. Hah. Sleep was farther than it had ever been. How could she trust him, how could she be sure he wouldn't desert her when she needed him?

Ruby's old pullout was about as comfortable as a bed of nails. She lay staring at the ceiling, more frightened and confused than she'd ever been.

She imagined going off with him to some cold marble

mansion in the East, far away from her mother and Ruby and Mona, far away from everything and everyone she knew. God, she'd miss them all. Even Mrs. Hodgkins seemed like a surrogate grandmother when Kate thought about leaving her.

Her life wasn't perfect, not by a mile, but at least it was familiar and predictable and safe.

Suddenly she couldn't stand lying there in pain and misery any longer. She hauled herself out of the pull-out, which groaned and squeaked before disgorging her from its lumpy depths with the painful poke of a popped spring.

Kate rubbed her bruised backside and silently dressed.

She arrived back at the duplex just after 3:00 a.m. It seemed forlorn and cheerless with moving boxes scattered around, most of the ornaments and books already packed away.

She walked into the bedroom and flopped on the bed

"What am I going to do?" she whispered to the ceiling. She curled up in a ball on the bare mattress, staring into the dark.

WELL, AS REUNIONS WENT, last night hadn't been a complete fiasco, Darren thought as he drove the quiet Sunday streets. The night hadn't ended the way his body had ached for it to end, but she hadn't slammed the door on his hopes, either.

If he knew anything for certain anymore, it was that he and Kate belonged together. When she'd told him about her father's death, quite a few things had begun to make sense.

"He lied to me," she'd said.

A big searchlight went on in his head when she'd said those words. It was like the moment when you discovered the source of a computer bug—that wonderful eureka moment that was the first step to solving the problem.

Not that Kate was like a computer—God, she was a lot more complex than that—but he had the key to her fear now, and her thing about lies. When it was just him and the computer, he always felt he had logic on his side. With Kate, he had to contend with emotions and feelings. He'd have a better chance winning at chess with Deep Blue than convincing the most stubborn, hot-tempered woman he'd ever known that she loved him.

He couldn't make her trust him. He hammered his hands against the wheel in frustration.

He drove aimlessly, thinking. He was willing to take a risk, couldn't she see that? What if, instead of asking her to trust him, he could show her how much *he* trusted *her*?

His heart began to pound. Why couldn't he show her he trusted her with his life?

He checked his mirrors and then jerked the wheel around for a U-turn. His blood hummed with anticipation as he headed the car in the direction of the duplex. She'd be home now, he was sure, now she didn't have to hide from him at her friend's place.

The car slowed as he entered the street where she lived. He felt suddenly dry-mouthed and hollow-bellied. What if he couldn't convince her?

Parking across the street, he marshaled his arguments. His palms were damp as he counted off on his fingers all the reasons why she should take a chance and trust him with her happiness.

In the end, he knew there was only one reason that counted. Did she love him? The answer to that question terrified him.

ACTION, THAT'S WHAT SHE needed. It was a lesson Kate had learned from her mother. "There are few problems that can't be solved with a scrub brush in your hand" her mother loved to say. Well, there was plenty of scrubbing and cleaning to be done before she moved at the end of the month. Kate scrutinized the small apartment. Sunshine streamed through dusty windows. That was a good place to start—with the windows.

Dragging one of the dining chairs over to the living room window, she climbed up, unhooking the drapes. She sneezed twice as dust tickled her nose. She pulled out the drapery hooks and piled the dirty drapes into her wicker laundry basket. She'd put the drapes on to wash now, then come back and wash the windows. She'd have the curtains washed and ironed and hanging over sparkling clean windows by nightfall.

Hiking the curtains into the laundry room, she crammed them into the washer and checked her watch. The washer would take about thirty minutes.

Back in her apartment, she tied her hair back out of the way and changed into old sweats and a T-shirt that had a hole in it. She put soap and vinegar into the bucket, added hot water and dug through the storage closet for her window washer.

She dipped the squeegee into the hot soapy water and began washing the windows. Up and down, then a swipe with the rubber end and the glass pane was clear. If only her fears could be cleared away as easily. She fell into a soothing rhythm, which allowed her thoughts free rein. They were anything but soothing.

She knew one thing now for certain.

She loved Darren. Whatever and whoever he was, she loved him.

And he'd come back for her.

But how could she trust him?

She remembered Ruby's words. "Be a grown-up, Kate" she'd said. Kate wasn't the girl she'd been half a year ago, when she'd seriously thought about spending her life with someone like Brian. She had grown up since then. It was Darren who'd helped her see who she really was, who'd encouraged her to take a risk and go back to school.

So what if she went with him and it didn't work? So what?

Swish up, swish down, squeak of rubber and on to the next strip.

She could always come back to Seattle, get another job. She'd be all right.

But if he broke her heart again, she didn't know if she could survive.

Back and forth her thoughts chased one another like the rubber swiper chasing drips down the window. He was going to phone today, and she had no idea what she was going to say to him.

She finished the last of the inside windows, emptied the bucket and dried her hands. She checked her watch. It was time to put the curtains in the dryer, then she could start on the outside of the windows. She stretched her arms over her head, rotating her shoulders, then headed back to the laundry room.

She stopped dead. Her heart lurched to her throat. There was a note taped to the washer. The cramped black sprawl as familiar as her own heartbeat.

Occupant of Apartment B,
Will you marry me?

Darren Edgar Kaiser

There was only one answer. It was time to trust her heart.

She looked around for a pen or pencil, anything to write with. The closest she could find to a writing implement was a dust-covered sliver of yellow soap lying in a corner.

Digging shaking hands in her sweatpants she pulled out an old lipstick and uncapped it. It was bright red. Perfect. She walked slowly over to the washer and wrote *Yes!* across the note in huge crooked letters, framing her answer in a thick, gooey red heart.

She felt his presence even before she turned around. "I hope you can read that far without your glasses," she teased, her voice husky through her tears.

"I have perfect vision. That's how I found you," he said softly.

"Kiss me, husband to be." She held her arms out, smiling through misty eyes.

He was quick to comply.

From *Matchmaker* magazine's October issue
Kaiser Meets His Match

Runaway Match of the Year, Darren Edgar Kaiser Jr., heir to the Kaiser Image Makers empire, is no longer missing. Sadly for this magazine and hopeful single women across the country, he's no longer a bachelor, either.

Darren Kaiser met his match, Kate Monahan Kaiser, on a recent trip to the West Coast.

The couple currently reside in Boston, where Kate attends university and Darren is working with a charitable education foundation to improve reading skills with a software program he developed.

eHARLEQUIN.com

The Ultimate Destination for Women's Fiction

Your favorite authors are just a click away
at www.eHarlequin.com!

- Take a sneak peek at the covers and
  read summaries of **Upcoming Books**

- Choose from over 600
  author **profiles!**

- Chat with your favorite authors
  on our **message boards.**

- Are you an author in the making?
  Get advice from published authors
  in **The Inside Scoop!**

**Learn about your favorite authors
in a fun, interactive setting—
visit www.eHarlequin.com today!**

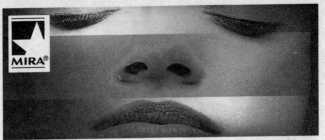

"Twisted villains, dangerous secrets…irresistible."
—*Booklist*

New York Times Bestselling Author

STELLA CAMERON

Just weeks after inheriting Rosebank, a once-magnificent Louisiana plantation, David Patin was killed in a mysterious fire, leaving his daughter, Vivian, almost bankrupt. With few options remaining, Vivian decides to restore the family fortunes by turning Rosebank into a resort hotel.

Vivan's dream becomes a nightmare when she finds the family's lawyer dead on the sprawling grounds of the estate. Suddenly Vivian begins to wonder if her father's death was really an accident…and if the entire Patin family is marked for murder.

Rosebank is not in Sheriff Spike Devol's jurisdiction, but Vivian, fed up with the corrupt local police, asks him for unofficial help. The instant attraction between them leaves Spike reluctant to get involved—until another shocking murder occurs and it seems that Vivian will be the next victim.

kiss them goodbye

"Cameron returns to the wonderfully atmospheric Louisiana setting…for her latest sexy-gritty, compellingly readable tale of romantic suspense."—*Booklist*

Available the first week of October 2004, wherever paperbacks are sold!

HARLEQUIN® *Blaze* ™

What could be a better combination than Sex & Candy?

Carrie Alexander's

upcoming Blaze books, of course!

#147 TASTE ME
August 2004

and

#163 UNWRAPPED
December 2004

Indulge in these two hot stories today!

On sale at your favorite retail outlet.